SON OF A BITCH, HE THOUGHT.

Four men—no, five—were rising up from the rocks with long guns in their hands. They were taking aim from cover, ready to cut down Jed and Nate, who still weren't expecting anything. They were damn fools to get so drunk that they had lost their caution.

There was no time for a warning and no certainty Jed and Nate would react the right way if he did shout to them in time.

Slocum palmed his Colt and snapped a shot at the nearest of the ambushers.

The gunshot brought hell into play . . .

OTHER BOOKS BY JAKE LOGAN

JAKE LOGAN

SLOCUM AND
THE LAW

BERKLEY BOOKS, NEW YORK

SLOCUM AND THE LAW

A Berkley Book / published by arrangement with
the author

PRINTING HISTORY
Berkley edition / May 1983

ISBN: 0-425-06153-1

A BERKLEY BOOK ® TM 757,375
Berkley Books are published by Berkley Publishing Corporation,
200 Madison Avenue, New York, N.Y. 10016.
The name ''BERKLEY'' and the stylized ''B'' with design are
trademarks belonging to Berkley Publishing Corporation.

PRINTED IN THE UNITED STATES OF AMERICA

1

John Slocum awoke and stretched, luxuriating in the feel of cool sheets against his bare skin and the warm length of woman at his side.

Slabs of lean muscle loosened on his tall frame and tendons creaked as they were tugged awake after a short night of deep rest. He yawned, and a narrow smile of satisfaction appeared on his darkly handsome face. His deep green eyes opened and he lolled his head to the side, away from the woman. His money belt lay undisturbed, draped over the back of a ladder-back chair in a far corner of the woman's bedroom.

Slocum felt a bone-deep contentment that sprang from many causes. The money belt and its contents was only one of them.

The belt held a comfortable heft of minted gold coins, taken not two weeks before from a payroll courier down Trinidad way. Enough money to buy a man one hell of a blowout in Kansas City, with some left over to stake him for the next roll of the dice— whatever and wherever that turned out to be.

There had been three of them in on it, enough to do the job and not a single split more. Each of the

other two had been carefully chosen by Slocum himself, and they were as closemouthed and cautious
afterward as he intended to be.

It had gone off exactly as Slocum had intended—a
picture-pretty operation that left the courier and the
lone shotgun guard alive, confused, and empty-handed.
It was always best that way, Slocum knew. Get
stupid and go to shooting, and someone was sure to
be mad enough to press the pursuit for days or even
weeks afterward. Do it right, and even the boys who
had been robbed would be content to let some damned
eastern insurance company worry about the loss.

They made their hit clean and quiet from the protection of a rocky overhang beside the courier's trail,
relieved the courier of the responsibility of the payroll, and were laughing their way up a little-known
trail into Raton Pass within minutes.

They made the split at the top of the pass and
separated there. It was not that Slocum disliked the
other men in the deal, it was simply that he preferred
to ride alone. So did they. If circumstances ever
brought them together again they would likely work
together again. It had been that kind of partnership.
In the meantime, each would go his own way.

Burt said he would be going south to El Paso del
Norte to spread his share of the money among some
brown-skinned girls. Petey intended to drift over toward Arizona to see what kind of trouble he could
get into there. He had heard there were some fair
possibilities in that growing territory.

Simply because the other two were riding south,

Slocum had chosen to turn around and drop back again through Raton. If Burt and Petey had been headed for Denver, say, John Slocum would have ridden south himself.

As it was, that happenstance decision turned out to have been the best one he had made lately.

He stretched and smiled again in the gray light of the early morning. He rolled his head to the other side and looked at the gleaming brown sprawl of hair on the pillow beside his and at the full-lipped loveliness of the face of the woman sleeping next to him.

Damned blind luck, he told himself. Damned *good* luck.

Three days before, he had stopped at an isolated homestead shack for water and a possible meal. He hadn't had then, and still did not have, any idea if he was still in Colorado or if he might have crossed the border into Kansas. It did not really matter.

What mattered was that Fay Bright was the owner of that homestead.

Fay was tall and slim almost to the point of scrawniness except for a massive jut of bosom beneath her much-washed housedress. Her pretty face had full lips and high cheekbones with shallow hollows beneath them. Her long brown hair was well brushed and left unpinned and full in utter disregard of current fashion. She had pale brown eyes which took on an almost golden hue when the light caught them in just the right way. She was something to look at, and she was a hell of a lot of woman in other ways as well.

It was common enough to find a lone woman trying to make a go of a homestead by herself after her man died or simply gave up the fight and left her. That was not at all Fay Bright's situation.

Miss Bright—she had never been married—had come out from Missouri alone, taken up land, and set in to work it. Her only explanation of that extraordinary act was that she was "tired of all the shit that's labeled expectations and respectability."

Fay was as direct in other ways as she was in that. She gave him the water he requested and when he asked if he could buy a meal she quoted a price without hesitation, cooked it, served it, and filled his belly. When Slocum stood to leave she gave him a head-to-toe scrutiny that left him feeling like a bull in an auctioneer's pen.

"Are you built all over as well as the exterior implies?" she had asked. "Or is that bulge down your leg just an empty promise?"

"Short on cash?" Slocum had drawled. His mind had been set on covering the ground between here and Kansas City, or he would not have answered so flippantly.

Fay clouded up and rained all over him. She took two long strides to cover the distance between them and launched a straight right shot to his chin. The carefully trimmed dark beard Slocum had taken to wearing lately was nowhere near enough padding to absorb the blow, and the punch damn well stung. Utter disbelief had kept him standing right there to take it.

"Damn, woman!" He reached up and rubbed his jaw, and she hit him again, this time in the stomach. There, at least, a slab of solid, corded muscle blocked the impact.

"Ouch, damn you!" She examined the knuckles of her right hand and shook it as if it hurt.

"If you'd learn to slap, like a lady, you wouldn't do that to yourself," Slocum said mildly. In spite of the attack, this woman had begun to intrigue him.

"If I'd slapped like a damn lady I couldn't have hurt you, you bastard. Don't you *ever* imply that I'm some kind of whore. I'm horny but I'm no whore."

"Yes, ma'am."

She shook her hand again. "You never answered my question," she accused.

Slocum grinned at her. "If that's an offer, I expect I'll accept it. You can judge the answer for yourself if I'm big enough to suit." He had been big enough to suit her, and she had damn sure been woman enough to suit him. That had been three days earlier, and if Slocum did not watch himself he might find himself liking this sort of luxury all too well. Fay Bright was simply one whole lot of woman.

He glanced at her again and saw that her eyes had opened. There was a gleam of dawning desire in the gold there. She smiled and reached out to press her fingertips against the point of his shoulder and turn him flat against the bed. Slocum grinned.

"Shut up, cowboy, I'm busy." His grin got wider.

Sometime during the first day, which they'd spent almost entirely in a cocoon of sweaty sheets, Fay seemed to have decided that John Slocum was a drifting cowboy in search of work. He had not bothered to correct her on the subject.

Fay pushed him down flat on his back and sat up. Her breasts were even more startling when they were free of the restraints of covering cloth. Her back was slender and flawless, and her rib cage showed sharp and clear above a flat plane of soft, slightly concave belly. Yet her breasts were enormous globes of taut, creamy flesh surmounted by broad disks of dark red nipple. Slocum was unsure of her age—she had not volunteered the information, nor had he asked—but the slight sag of those glorious tits suggested that she was approaching or might already have reached her thirties.

She shook her head, and that long spill of brown hair curled and flowed like the waves in the blue Gulf of Mexico which Slocum had admired a time or two in the past. She arched her back to take deliberate advantage of that impressive jut of breast and gave him a coquettish smile.

Just as deliberately, just as provocatively, Fay looked him in the eye and slowly moistened the fullness of her lips.

Slocum faked a yawn, closed his eyes, and laced his fingers behind his neck. He pretended disinterest and willed the massive pole at his crotch not to betray him by springing to attention.

"You can't do it, cowboy."

Slocum faked another yawn.

"You'll see."

Slocum felt the bed shift slightly as she moved. A moment later he could feel the faint, delicate, whispering touch of her hair as she leaned over him.

The soft tendrils of fine-spun hair dragged lightly, so lightly that he was not entirely sure he was feeling them, across his belly and down to his balls. Slocum clenched his teeth. That damned, unreliable, mind-of-its-own son of a bitch he carried between his legs was beginning to pulse and engorge itself.

Fay laughed with delight. He could feel the soft hair fall more heavily on him now, and Fay's breath was warm against his flesh.

His pecker came throbbingly erect in spite of Slocum's best intentions, and bobbed repeatedly against her cheek. Fay laughed again.

"Bitch," Slocum said affectionately.

"You're just jealous because I won," she said lightly, taking no offense.

Slocum opened his eyes and raised his head in time to see her dip her head and engulf him in her mouth. Her cheeks hollowed as she applied a strong suction to him, and the heat of her mouth was intense.

Slocum sighed. "You're a bitch, Miss Bright, but I will admit that you're talented."

She disengaged long enough to say, "That's what I like about you, cowboy. You always tell me the nicest things." She grinned and went back to what she had been doing.

Slocum was a beaten man, and he knew it. He closed his eyes, lay back, and let Fay have her way with him. What a way for her to have her way.

After several delightful minutes she noisily released him with a loud slurp and gurgle. "This isn't all going to be one-way, cowboy," she said.

He felt the bed shift again and she planted one long, smooth thigh on either side of Slocum's hips. She ran her fingers lightly over him for a few seconds, honoring and enjoying the marble-hard length of him, then guided him into her body as she lowered herself over his pole. Slocum felt himself sink deep into her and Fay sighed. "Nice, cowboy. Damn nice."

"Uh-huh," he mumbled. He really was not interested in conversation at the moment. When he opened his eyes Fay was bending forward and his entire field of vision was filled by the sight of those immense bouncing boobs. They swayed back and forward with the rhythm of her body as she pumped him in and out in long, slow strokes. Slocum could feel the building heat of an approaching climax. "You ready soon?" he asked.

"Maybe not for days," she said. "This feels *so* good."

"The hell with that noise." Slocum reached up to palm one dangling breast. It overflowed his hand and was softer than any pillow. He pushed upward and to the side, levered her over so that she slipped away from him and fell sprawling onto the bed beside him with her legs flung apart. "Uh-huh," he said. "Just like that."

With catlike speed Slocum rolled over on top of her and pinned her to the bed. He paused only briefly to get his bearings and plunged himself full depth into her as hard as he could. Fay's breath caught in her throat and her arms wrapped around him. She raised her legs and locked her heels above and behind him. "You're a real bastard, cowboy."

Slocum was not talking. He bucked and drove without restraint, slamming the hard hammer of his belly against the softness of hers in a frenzy of constantly accelerating motion until the heat that was in him reached the boiling point and spewed splashing and pulsing into her.

Distantly he was aware that Fay had begun to shudder and buck right along with him and at the last moment she seemed to pass out.

Spent, Slocum let himself fall on top of her, letting the woman take his weight as he gasped for breath. Fay blinked and shook her head. She seemed to be returning from someplace very far away. She held him closer.

"Damn, cowboy," she whispered. "I didn't think I was going to do that after all the times last night." She chuckled. "You're pure hell in the saddle, you know it?"

Slocum laughed and rolled off her. The cool morning air felt chill and cleansing when it struck the patches of fresh sweat on his chest and belly. He could feel a trickle of lingering wetness sliding cold and sticky on his leg.

Fay shuddered once, sat up, and smiled at him. She attested to her joy with a flick of her tongue and a laugh of pleasure. "A cigar now, maybe?"

Slocum nodded.

She brought him the stogie, scratched a match aflame, and held it for him. When he had it going she began to build a fire in the stove and, naked, went about the routine of putting a pot of water on the stove to boil for coffee along with an iron skillet to start their breakfast.

"I reckon I could do the decent thing now," Slocum said.

"What's that?"

"Get my butt up outta this bed and do the morning chores."

She shook her head. "I've been doing them every morning since I got here. I'll have to do them myself when you're gone. I can do them this morning too."

Slocum clamped his teeth around the moist tip of his cigar and grinned.

This must be what everybody's always talking about when they say they got it made, he thought. Belt full of gold and a hot and pretty woman who don't mind doing for a man. Now *that* is having it made.

He drew deep on his cigar, closed his eyes, and listened to the sounds of the woman doing for him.

Uh-huh, he thought. Got it made.

He should have known it wouldn't last.

2

"Don't be such a stick-in-the-mud, John. I'm not offering you charity, you know. I really could use the help if you'd agree to stay on for a while." Fay Bright guided her light buckboard up the side of a small rise toward a nest of pale red rocks jutting up from the baked earth and pulled the cold-blooded cob drawing it to a halt near the crest of the low hill. "Besides," she said, "I have an ulterior motive."

Slocum swallowed a small smile and got out of the rig to hitch the patient horse to an iron weight. There were no trees or even bushes in this arid country to tie the horse to. Fay still believed that Slocum was a cowboy looking for work, and for the past two days she had been trying to offer him employment.

He had not corrected her idea that the reason he was declining the offer was because she was not raising cattle on her quarter section of "free" land. Slocum knew, and probably Fay did too, that there was no such thing as a free lunch—not from a saloon, and certainly not from the damned government.

"Goats really aren't so bad, you know," Fay said as she gathered her skirts in one hand and led him the

11

few yards up to the top of the low hill. "I am not so foolish as to think a person—man or woman—or even a family can successfully farm out here. I did a lot of asking before I made my decision to come here. A farmer can make a crop probably one year in eight without irrigation here. Those are poor odds indeed."

Slocum nodded. He had seen the dry-land farmers come, and just as often he had seen them go. They came believing everything the land agents had told them and they left knowing the truth. Usually the only thing they left behind was a pile of scrap lumber someone else would use for firewood, lumber that used to be a shack intended for living in, and a plowed scar on the natural grass which might never recover. This was country for livestock, Slocum knew, not for farmers.

"And a hundred sixty acres will support—what? —three cows here? Something like that, I would think. A few more if the homestead has a creek bottom on it. Fewer in some places."

"About three," Slocum agreed.

"Right," Fay said forcefully. "Three cows. A person is not going to earn a living from three cows."

Slocum nodded.

"The obvious answer," she said firmly, "is goats." She reached the low ring of rocks, brushed the top of the nearest, and sat on it. She motioned for him to sit beside her.

"Goats," she said with conviction. "They don't need nearly so much grass as a cow. They give meat, milk, cheese, and mohair: all cash commodities. You can graze five goats on the grass one cow requires and earn twenty-five times as much income from that graze. Believe me, I thought it out quite carefully. And there is no disgrace, John, in raising goats."

"I know that," he said.

Fay nodded her satisfaction with his response. "Of course, a quarter section is still too little to do really well, even with goats."

"Uh-huh," Slocum muttered. The slanting evening sun was highlighting Fay's long hair. The effect was quite fetching. So was the way the light outlined the faint hint of golden down on her hollowed cheek and caught the curve of her eyelashes. Damn, she was a pretty woman. He looked thoughtfully at the swell of her bosom. Knowing exactly what riches lay beneath that cloth made it all the more tempting to touch her. He reached out and cupped one breast. She smiled when he squeezed her there and rolled a firming nipple between his fingertips.

"In a minute, John. Let me finish first." She let him know it was a delay and not a rejection by resting her hand on his crotch, idly massaging him through the rough cloth of his jeans while she spoke. "Right about here," she said, "is the end of my filing. About four rods west of where we are sitting actually."

Slocum nodded. His attention really was not concentrated on anything she was saying. His hand moved more insistently on her breast.

"In a minute, dear," she repeated. "What I was thinking, John, was that a person might take up this next quarter section west and—well—enter a partnership, so to speak."

She gave him a sharp look of impatience. "Are you paying attention to me, John?"

"Uh-huh." He wasn't.

"Men!" she said with obvious exasperation. "If you aren't actually *in* someplace warm and wet, you're *looking* for a place to put it." She gave him a painfully hard squeeze which finally succeeded in capturing his attention. "Did you hear what I said, John?"

"Mmmm. Maybe you ought to say it again. To make sure I got it right the first time."

Fay shook her head, but she laughed at the same time. "All right. What I was suggesting was that you might file a homestead claim on that quarter section out there." She waved in a generally westerly direction. "All you would have to do would be to file on it. I could stock it. And, of course, we would share living expenses." She grinned. "Not to mention the bed we've already been sharing. If you have any complaints, you've been very gentlemanly about not expressing them." She gave him a mock-serious look and a much more gentle squeeze. "Do you have any complaints, John?"

"About as many as you've admitted." It had only been a few hours since the last time he had taken her, but already he was feeling as randy as a fifteen-year-old boy sniffing after his first woman.

"Then you'll think about what I'm suggesting? I know it isn't a cattle spread, but . . ."

"I'll think about it," he said, just to shut her up.

Actually, John Slocum startled himself. The truth was that he *was* thinking about her offer a hell of a lot more seriously than he ever would have believed possible.

Homesteading was for rubes and suckers. Slocum *knew* that. But Fay Bright was as strong and independent in her thinking as she was vigorous in bed. A man could do a lot worse than to take up with her.

A drifting man with a fast gun and too widespread a reputation gets into the habit of thinking there can be no other kind of life for him—that all he can do is keep on moving until some little bastard with a reward poster in his back pocket and no qualms about backshooting puts an end to things with a nester's shotgun and a pine box. Or until some hick sheriff and a dozen of his half-drunk buddies get lucky some night. Until the mainspring on the Colt breaks and some slick-haired gambler with a sleeve gun puts a lead pellet in his guts. Until an exhilarating run turns sour and a horse steps into a prairie-dog hole with a posse half a mile behind. Until any number of stupid things might happen.

A man accepts that as part of the game and learns to live it one hour at a time. This hour, this moment, might be all that a hard man has.

Fast money, fast horses and fast women: he learns to think of those as all there is.

But . . . he glanced toward Fay again. Damn, she

was fine-looking. As good a lover as a man might hope to find. Didn't make any attempt to rope and brand a fellow. Hell, she hadn't even mentioned marriage when she was making her pitch. Just file on the land and move right in.

A man couldn't ask for anything more and sure ought to expect a hell of a lot less.

Slocum shook his head. He couldn't really believe the way he was thinking all of a sudden. If Burt or Petey had suggested something like this to him when they were making their split and heading off their separate ways, he would have laughed at them—or punched them.

As if she knew exactly what he was thinking, Fay smiled. "You don't have to be in any hurry to decide," she said. "The offer is open. It's just a suggestion, after all. In the meantime . . ." She stood and began to unbutton her dress.

The outcropping of red rocks formed almost a complete circle around a low-walled nest of spiky grass and loose gravel. Fay slipped out of her dress— she was wearing nothing beneath it—and stood tall and slim and proud in the red-gold rays of late sun. She spread her dress on the hard soil and lay on top of it, waiting while Slocum shucked his clothes and lowered himself on top of her.

He was hard and ready, throbbing with his need for her, but she reached between their bodies and held him, lightly caressing the length of him as she pulled his weight down on top of her.

"Let me feel it there between us for just a moment, please. I love the feel of it, you know.'' She laughed. ''I've seen mares bred by stallions that weren't hung as well as you are, dear.''

Slocum pressed himself down onto her, his cock caught between his belly and hers, throbbing insistently for its release. Fay drew her hands out from between their bodies and wrapped herself around Slocum's muscular length. The gravel soil must have cut into her back and buttocks, but she gave no sign of discomfort. Sharp-edged bits of gravel pricked Slocum's knees, but he was unwilling to move off her.

In less than a minute Fay began to move her hips beneath him. Her breath came quicker in her slender throat and she reached to push his hips up and guide him back down again, this time into the wet heat of her ready body.

A low groan slid through her lips as she took him into her, and when he began to move she matched him stroke for stroke.

He stiffened and lunged one final time and dropped, spent, onto the soft cushion of her breasts.

''A quarter inch,'' she said softly. ''One quarter inch more and I could have tasted that on the back of my tongue.'' She chuckled into his ear. ''In fact, dear, I think I *would* like to taste that. The next time. All right?''

''I'm a decent fella,'' Slocum said. ''Reckon I'll allow it.''

Fay laughed. ''You *are* good to me, John.''

"I'd deny it, but I can't. It's the simple damn truth."

"Now if you would be good enough to move, sir, there is a particularly nasty rock poking me where only you should be allowed to poke me."

"Always the gentleman, that's me," Slocum said lightly. He took his weight on his hands and began to lift away from her.

A sound beyond their little nest of rock and grass chilled him and he froze in the awkward position while his mind raced to assess distance and direction.

It was a footfall he had heard. His holstered Colt was within reach, but barely so. The Colt was *there*. The sound had come from *there*.

Another faint crunch of soil under a boot sole.

Slocum launched himself in a rolling dive to the right. His hand unerringly found the use-polished grips of his gun. The roll ended with Slocum on his knees, his back against solid red rock, Colt cocked without conscious effort and aimed toward the source of the sounds.

"What . . .?" Slocum was scarcely aware that the woman had spoken.

He was completely aware of the suddenly pale, fuzzily boyish face of the youngster who had been walking up the hill toward them.

"My God, mister, don't shoot!" the boy cried. He threw his hands into the air. His voice was quavering with terror.

"Shit!" Slocum said.

He could see now that the kid would be barely into

his teens, if he was that old. His britches were much patched, and his suspenders were just pieces of twine strung over his shoulders and tied to his belt loops. His hat looked as if it had been used as the doormat in front of a very busy place. He for damn sure was not armed, unless he was carrying a Barlow knife in his pocket. Judging from the kid's appearance, Slocum thought that even that common item of juvenile wealth would be absent.

"It's all right, kid. You can put your hands down."

"Yes, sir."

"And turn around, please."

"Sir?"

"Turn around. Face the other way is what I want you to do. I'll tell you when you can turn back this way."

"Yes, sir." The boy hurried to do exactly what he had been told.

Slocum stood and helped Fay to her feet before he shoved his Colt back into its holster and began pulling his clothes on.

"Sir?" The boy was still facing toward Fay's buckboard.

"Yes?"

"I come up here looking for Miss Bright, sir. I got a message for her."

Fay finished buttoning her dress. She gave her hair a quick shake and stroked it with her hands. She waited for Slocum to get into his shirt before she spoke. "It's all right, Andy. You can turn around now."

"Yes, ma'am." The kid was blushing furiously when he finally did turn. He faced toward them but seemed to find something of great interest to look at on the ground immediately in front of his toes. "I didn't mean . . ."

"I know that, Andy. It's all right. Believe me," she said.

"Yes, ma'am." He was still examining the ground.

Fay laughed and left the circle of rocks to walk to him. She lifted his chin on her fingers until he was looking at her. "Disappointed?"

"No, ma'am, I . . ." He stopped and swallowed hard. The look he gave her was anguished. The glance he sent over her shoulder toward Slocum, who was still buttoning his shirt, was raw envy. "Yes'm, maybe some."

"That's all right, Andy. You're entitled to your feelings, you know, whatever they happen to be. I'm sorry if I disappointed you, Andy, but I'm entitled to my feelings too. And I don't make any apologies for anything I do." She laughed. "Maybe your folks are right about me after all. But, personally, I still don't believe it. You can if you like."

"No, ma'am." He gave her a smile—a small one, but genuine. "No, ma'am, I expect I still don't think that. You been too good to me for me to ever think bad of you."

"Thank you, Andy. Now, what was this message you were supposed to bring me?"

"Oh." He gave her an odd, almost sorrowful

look. "The sheriff asked me to bring it out to you, ma'am, an' I seen your buggy up here and . . ."

"That is all right, Andy. What's the message?"

Andy looked uncomfortable. He fished in the pocket of his trousers and brought out a crumpled piece of paper. Slocum guessed from its color that it was a telegraph message form.

"I'm awful sorry, ma'am," he said as he handed it to her. He turned and took a few steps downhill, stopped, and swung around to look Fay in the eyes again. "Ma'am?"

"Yes, Andy?"

"I won't be saying anything bad about you in town, ma'am. You can count on that. I wouldn't never."

"Thank you, Andy."

The boy moved on downhill to a decrepit nag he had tied to a wheel of the buckboard. The pony carried no saddle and wore a sawed-off driving bit for a bridle.

Fay unfolded the paper. Her shoulders sagged when she read the message. Slocum moved down to stand beside her and put an arm around her slim waist.

"Bad news?"

She had begun to cry. She nodded, paying no attention to the tears that were beginning to roll down her cheeks. John Slocum was no hand when it came to comforting women. He did not know what to do here. "What is it, Fay?"

Instead of answering she thrust the telegram into his hand. The message was simple enough.

WILLIAM BRIGHT ARRESTED HERE THIS
DATE ON CAPITAL MURDER CHARGE
STOP TRIAL APPROXIMATELY FOUR
WEEKS STOP PLEASE ACKNOWLEDGE
NOTIFICATION OF NEXT OF KIN STOP

It was signed Rolfe Kuner, marshal of Trinidad.

"William Bright?" Slocum asked.

"My brother."

"I'm sorry about this, Fay."

She nodded and used both hands to wipe the tears
away. "I have to go to him, John."

It was Slocum's turn to nod.

"I don't know what this is all about, John, but I
do know that William could never have killed anyone. This . . . this isn't right. It can't be."

"You oughta know, I guess, that this marshal
likely wouldn't've gone to the trouble of notifying
you this way if it wasn't pretty certain that William is
gonna hang, Fay. For that matter, most laws I've
known wouldn't go to any trouble regardless. But
this way—well, I reckon you should prepare yourself
for bad news."

The tears were running again. "You might be
right. But I *know* he couldn't have kill anyone."

"Fay, that's a thing no one knows. Not really.
Things happen that a man doesn't plan on. There
isn't always a choice in the matter."

"You don't know William."

"No, I don't. And you don't know whatever is
behind this charge. I'm not saying you're wrong.

I'm just saying you should prepare yourself. You understand?''

She nodded and wiped her eyes again. "John, could I ask a great favor of you?''

"Of course.''

"Could you . . . come with me? To Trinidad?''

Slocum sighed and rubbed at the fur on his face. A week before he had been in Trinidad robbing a payroll. If he went back now he stood a better than fair chance of being recognized and joining William Bright in Marshal Kuner's jail.

"Please?''

"If we travel down there together it wouldn't do your reputation any good,'' he said, avoiding a direct answer.

Fay snorted. "It isn't all that much of a reputation to begin with. And I care about it even less than that.''

"I'm thinking about your brother, too,'' he invented. Not that it was a bad point he had come up with on the spur of the moment. "If you are going to help William any, you might need public opinion on your side. You don't know yet what you're going to have to work with.''

She thought about that a moment. "We wouldn't have to be staying together openly. But if you could just be where I could see you now and then.'' Her face twisted into something that was close to a smile although it missed the mark somewhat. "Look at me, will you? I take such damned pride in being my own woman. Now a little trouble comes along and the first thing I do is grab at a man to lean on. Silly, aren't I?''

"No," Slocum said softly. "There's men and there's women. There's also friends. I expect we've come to be friends here lately, atop of everything else. I guess it ain't wrong for you to look to a friend when there's trouble.'' He swallowed hard and added, ''I reckon I could hang around on the fringes down there. Maybe see if there's anything I could do to help.''

The promise was out of his mouth before he realized his intention to make it. He should have regretted it at once, immediately recanted, and taken it back. He did not.

It was a fool thing to say and a worse thing to do. But, hell, he was going to do it.

Fay Bright had sparked a hope in him that he had never expected to have again. That was something right there. No matter what else he did, however things turned out, that right there was a gift she had given him, without ever knowing what she had done.

It was a gift he might somehow be able to repay now.

And, hell, he could shave his beard. No one down that way had seen him without it. That would be some protection right there.

And, as he had come to know right well when he was planning that little job, there was just a world of hideout possibilities back in the mountains south of Trinidad. A man could hole up in the hills and not be seen or heard from until or unless he wanted to be. He could shave and kind of keep out of sight and nose around amongst the boys who would be likely to know the straight stuff on whatever this murder was that William Bright was accused of doing. He might be able to do Fay a whole lot of good that way. A man never knows until he tries.

And if someone should happen to connect him with the recent robbery, he could get on his horse and light out from there as easily as from here. The loss would be the same from one as from the other.

Meantime, he could give Fay Bright a little bit of hope, just like she'd unknowingly given him.

Yeah, he thought, that would be all right.

If he was careful. If he was lucky. He knew he could be careful, and luck was something he was always willing to court.

"I'll do what I can," he repeated.

The look on the woman's face was enough to make the stupid promise damn near worthwhile.

3

John Slocum was not used to gestures of affection. Years of hard living and his own dark good looks had given him more than his share of experience with women, but little of that had had to do with the softer side of their affections. Screwing, yes, but not gentle, genuine caring. He was startled, then, and oddly pleased when at the railroad depot Fay came onto her tiptoes to give him a chaste kiss goodbye. In a way it seemed more stirring than a grind against his crotch could have been.

"William has a cabin of some sort on the edge of town. He's written me about it. I'll probably be staying there, John, or possibly at the hotel. Try the cabin first. And do be careful."

He nodded. That obviously concerned caution was also something beyond his normal experience. "You have enough money?" he asked her.

"I'm sure I do," she said. On the drive to town Slocum had stripped a handful of bright yellow double eagles from his money belt and pressed them on her. "Lawyers aren't trusting people," he had warned her. "They know too much about folks for that. You'll

27

need the fee up front.'' Fay had accepted the money and thanked him without protest. It was as if, Slocum noted, she had already accepted him into the partnership she had proposed and now was thinking in those terms rather than separate identities.

He handed her up the steel steps into the passenger coach and felt oddly alone when the hissing, steaming train pulled away. The drive back to Fay Bright's homestead intensified his sense of being alone. Yet riding alone was the only way Slocum knew. His awareness of it now was disquieting.

At the homestead he went swiftly through the chores that were necessary to leave the place vacant for a week or more.

Kids that had been confined in a weaning pen were turned back onto the grass. With any luck they would return to their dams and suck again, taking care of their own feeding and at the same time eliminating the need to worry about daily milkings for the does.

Slocum looked at the small herd—flock? he wondered; he could not remember which term it should be—and shook his head. He looked at the palm of his powerful right hand, perfectly accustomed to the feel of a Colt's curving butt, and with a short laugh wondered if a hand like that could fit on a damned goat's teat. The idea seemed ludicrous.

He turned Fay's harness horse onto the grass, stowed harness, bridle, and tugs under cover, and dumped a convenient assortment of foods into a sack he could tie behind his cantle. He was used to traveling with less comfort than that. He had certainly done it often enough.

It was still only midday when he was done with everything he could think of that might need doing. He remembered to pull the door closed when he was ready to leave but to leave it unlocked. Someone might need to come in and make use of the place while they were away. Peaceful, trusting thinking like that was something he would have to make a conscious effort to adjust to if he should decide to take Fay up on her suggestion.

He mounted the leggy, deep-chested silver roan he had bought over in Durango and reined the beast toward the southwest, back toward Trinidad and possible trouble.

He found the wagon late in the afternoon of the next day. The stupid bastard who was driving it had pulled the wheels off a low drop into a shallow wash, square onto a half-buried rock. Good tire rims and properly tended wheels still might have let him get away with the mistake, but a combination of iron rims worn thin and dry, brittle spokes had given the man a broken wheel. As might have been expected from a sorry bastard who appeared in public wearing bib overalls, he had no spare wheel.

"Sure am glad you came along, mister," the farmer said when Slocum was near enough to speak to without shouting. "We can use the help."

Slocum pulled the roan to a halt out of a sense of

amazement rather than duty. "Hell," he said, "I didn't know I'd offered any."

A pair of women came fluttering excitedly out of the wagon, and Slocum decided he could stop long enough to look anyway. He hooked a knee over his saddle horn and fished in his pockets for a cigar and a match.

"You wouldn't have any of those to spare, would you, mister?" the farmer asked.

"Nope." Slocum took his time about building a satisfactory coal at the tip of the cigar, then flipped his spent match into the sandy draw where the farmer's wagon had broken down.

The women who were reaching them now looked like mother and daughter. The mother was a stubby balloon of dried leather in a dress made shapeless by her shapeless body. How a man could stand to bed down with the likes of that night after night was more than Slocum could understand.

The daughter, on the other hand, wasn't entirely bad. She was of marrying age—call it eighteen or a bit less—and ripe. She had flaming red hair pinned under a floppy bonnet, and while her dress was no more attractive or fashionable than her mother's it was doing a poor job of hiding the points and curves underneath the faded cloth.

She was freckled and cute as a bug's ear and, Slocum noticed with a tingle south of his beltline, had a way of batting her eyelashes that hinted her flower had been plucked more than once already.

"Yep," the farmer said, "we sure are lucky you happened along so's you could help us here."

Slocum gave him a cold look. He'd already told the silly bastard once. That ought to be enough for any man.

"We're *very* grateful," the girl added. She sidled back behind her mother, so her folks couldn't see, and added a few statements with her eyes.

Sure looked to be ripe, Slocum thought. He could feel the heat gnawing at his groin.

The girl took a deep breath and wet her lips. Slocum kicked free of the left stirrup and let himself slide down off the saddle. "Reckon I could stand somebody else's cooking tonight, after all."

"Good. Good. We knowed you'd help." The farmer stepped up to wring Slocum's hand with more enthusiasm than was necessary. He kept on shaking it. "I'm Chester Berry. That's my ol' woman there, and the girl is our youngest, called Cherry. All the others've grown an' gone. Don't know what we'll do when the baby's gone too." He kept on shaking Slocum's hand until Slocum forcibly pulled it away.

Cherry Berry? Slocum thought. They should have named her Raz. If she were dark they could have called her Black. But maybe those names were already taken by some of the older Berry offspring. Looking at Chester, Slocum would not have been surprised.

Chester seemed to be waiting for something. Slocum finally figured out what it was. "You can call me John," he said.

"What's your last name, John?" Chester reached to try and shake some more. Slocum pretended not to see.

"Chester, there's some things a man don't ask out here. A name's one of them."

"Right. Sure. Whatever you say, John." He grinned. "We got a lot to learn, I expect. Just comin' out from Ioway, we are. Lookin' for opportunity. Land of opportunity out here, the way we hear it. Lost our farm back home. Poor soil, you know. Couldn't get a decent crop no matter how hard a man worked. Poor soil."

"I've heard that about Iowa," Slocum said with a straight face.

"You heard right, then. But we figure to do lots better out here. Heard a man can make his fortune farmin' this virgin soil."

"That's what they say," Slocum agreed. It wasn't a lie. He *had* heard some shyster land agents say it. Of course, *they* had been lying, but that was their worry.

"How's about you give us a hand with this busted wheel, John, while my old woman fixes us a supper fit for hard-workin' men?" He waved his wife away with a shake of his wrist. The girl, Slocum noticed, stayed where she was. Her father was not looking her way, and she was making no bones about admiring the bulge at Slocum's crotch.

Slocum took a pull on his cigar and removed it from his jaw so he could inspect the length of ash building on it. "I don't suppose you have any ideas on how that oughta be done?"

"Not right off," Chester agreed, "but I reckon we can study on it some."

Slocum grunted. "I saw some drifted wood 'bout half a mile farther up this wash. I expect you could take one of those mules an' drag a chunk down to use as a skid till you get to the next town."

"There's a town nearby, John?"

He shrugged. "Twenty, twenty-five miles, as close as I can recall. I'll point you the way in the morning."

"Good. That's real good, John. I—uh—don't s'pose you could ride back up to where you seen that drifted wood and pull some back with your rope, could you?"

Slocum inspected his cigar again. "I'd be real happy to do that, Chester, but this old horse of mine, he buggers real bad if you try to rope off him. Feels a rope along his flank, he just goes plumb crazy. Wouldn't be safe to use him."

"Oh." Chester looked disappointed. "Well . . ."

The truth was that Slocum had never used a rope off the roan, so he might not have been lying, exactly. On the other hand, he had bought the horse from a rancher who had been proud of the animal's abilities working cattle. Slocum's interest lay with his durable qualities for covering ground, though, and he had not paid a whole lot of attention to the seller's praise when it came to other work.

Since Slocum did not offer to undertake the chore for him, Chester gloomily turned to the task of unhitching his off mule and leading it up the wash bottom toward the promised wood.

Slocum watched him go, shaking his head in near disbelief—although he was willing to believe things about Chester Berry that he would not have about other men. He was leading the mule instead of riding it. And the silly son of a bitch was making man and mule both walk in the deep sand instead of mounting the much firmer wash bank and at least walking in relative comfort.

No wonder ol' Chester hadn't been able to make a crop in Iowa dirt, Slocum thought.

"Would you like some coffee, John?"

"I reckon."

Cherry gave him a smile and a wink that were anything but shy and trotted off toward the evening fire her mother had started.

Wonderful folks, the Berrys, Slocum thought. Salt of the earth and all that crap. He shook his head again.

He led the roan past the Berry wagon to a patch of reasonably thick grass, pulled his saddle, and slipped the hobbles on the horse. There was a standing seep in the wash floor where the animal could drink, so he knew it would not be far come daylight. He thought about laying out his bedroll and rifle ready for the night but decided against that. With a silly bastard like Chester in the neighborhood he might want to move his gear come nightfall. Slocum was not entirely sure the man was not faking his stupidity. It seemed difficult to believe that a man could reach maturity and still be so dumb.

"Here you are, John." Cherry was holding two tin cups of coffee with a bit of rag wrapped around the handle of each to keep from burning herself.

"Thanks." Slocum accepted the brew—it was weak enough that he could see the bottom of the cup, he noticed—and hunkered down next to his saddle.

"Mind if I join you?"

"Nope."

Cherry sat on the ground with her feet apart and the hem of her dress riding up. It was not exactly a ladylike pose, and she was not wearing any drawers. There was curly red hair instead of cloth on view down there. Slocum took his time about looking it over. Cherry grinned at him.

"Cherry, huh?" Slocum asked.

"It's my name."

"Interesting." Slocum took a sip of the coffee. It might have been weak but it was damn sure hot.

"Momma and Pa sleep heavy," the girl said.

"I don't."

"Interesting," she mimicked.

"John!" The call came from far up the wash.

"Sounds like your pa is back," Slocum said.

"See you later?"

"I'll be somewhere around here when I bed down," he said.

Cherry licked her lips and batted her eyes at him. She came lightly onto her feet and raced back toward the wagon, where her mother was doing something over the fire.

Interesting, Slocum thought to himself. And ripe.

He took his time about finishing his coffee and walking back up to the broken-down wagon.

Chester at least had managed to luck onto a length of wood that would do the job that was needed, although he seemed unsure of how to go about the task of fitting it under the wagon bed as a drag.

With a sigh of weary resignation, Slocum used Berry's axe to trim the weathered cottonwood branch. It was easier to do it himself than to try to explain to Berry how it should be done. He directed its placement and lashing under the wheelless axle end. Somehow Slocum was not amazed to discover that he was the one doing the lifting when the time came for that.

"Salt of the earth," Slocum muttered to himself.

"Huh?" the farmer asked.

"Nothing," Slocum said. "Nothing at all."

4

Slocum pushed his soogan aside, sat up in the pale hint of starlight, and belched. The second time too, supper tasted lousy. He grimaced. Food fit for a working man, eh? If Mrs. Berry screwed as well as she cooked it was a wonder they had had more than one kid. Slocum had slopped hogs with better than that.

A cigar would have helped take the taste out of his mouth; he certainly wanted one badly enough. But there are some things a prudent man does not do, and showing a light at night when there are strangers within gunshot is one of them. And so far he could find no reason to show either trust or affection to Chester Berry.

That daughter of theirs was another matter altogether. Cherry Berry did seem to show some promise.

Thinking of promises . . . implied if not exactly stated . . . he sat silently in the night, quelling his desire for a smoke with thoughts about the ripeness of the girl's body, his patience a long-practiced habit now after so many years of cultivating it. Patience was another thing a man learned if he expected to survive as John Slocum had had to do through the years.

After a time, probably an hour and a half after the Berry family had bedded down beside their partially repaired wagon, he could hear the approaching swish of feet moving through grass. Slocum thought he knew who it would be, but his Colt came naturally to his hand and his thumb fell automatically over the cold steel of its hammer. If there was going to be any surprises in the neighborhood, he would prefer to be the one who delivered them.

"John?" The girl's whisper came to him softly.

"Here," he whispered back. He continued to hold the blue steel Colt.

She came to the sound of his voice. When she was a few paces away he could see that it was Cherry. "You moved your bedroll. I almost didn't find you."

"Softer over here," he said in a low tone. There seemed no point in getting into a discussion of the real reason.

"Oh." She giggled. "Now that I found you . . ."

Cherry stood at the foot of his soogan. In a single motion she pulled her dress over her head and dropped it to the grass.

The starlight was faint, but it was enough.

Her body was as ripe and full as its promise. Breasts almost as large as Fay's but standing firmer and higher than the older woman's. Hips a wide swell below a slightly thick waist. In a few more years, Cherry Berry would be unattractively plump and sagging. For the moment, her flesh still had the tautness of youth.

There was too little light for him to see the rich red color of her unbound hair. In the starlight her bright red patch of curly pubic hair was a swatch of darkness against pale flesh.

"Like what you see?" she asked.

"I've seen worse."

Cherry giggled. "You aren't one for wild compliments, are you?"

"Nope."

She swished her hips and made several turns back and forth in front of him. "A girl likes to be told she's pretty, you know."

"I've heard that," Slocum agreed. "I thought you came over here because you wanted to screw. If you just want to tease, go back to bed." He lay back down in his bedroll and waited for the silly little bitch to make up her mind. There was room for her beside him, but if she thought he was going to beg for it, piss on her.

"John?"

"Mmmm?"

"You aren't like most men, are you?"

"I wouldn't know about that. I ain't never been most men."

She dropped to her knees at the foot of the soogan and crept forward to lie beside him. "I've never been with anybody like you before. Older and experienced and everything."

"It's the everything that'll get you, kid," he said. He was not entirely sure if this girl excited him or was just making him feel old before his time.

"You do want me, don't you, John?" Her right hand found his crotch, and she began to lick his neck below his ear.

"Sure," he said. Physically he certainly did. He had a hard-on so insistent he would have been willing to screw a prairie-dog hole if Cherry wasn't around.

She felt the size of the throbbing pain and gasped. "Golly, I didn't know they came so big!" She nibbled on his ear some more and giggled again. "Love me?"

"Nope," he said.

Cherry sighed. "You do want me, though?"

"Uh-huh."

Her fingers skillfully freed him from the restraint of buttons, and she sat up to help pull his jeans and drawers down. She fondled him with both hands. "So big," she said.

"Gobble it," he told her.

"What's that?"

"French style."

"I don't know what you mean."

Damned if she didn't sound like she meant it. "Are you serious, girl?"

"Of course."

"Nobody ever gave you French lessons?"

"No. I've never known anybody but some Ioway farm boys. Most of them could barely talk American, much less French."

Slocum laughed in spite of himself. "It doesn't have anything to do with talking, Cherry. It means you should take it in your mouth and suck on it."

She gave him a look of disgust.

Slocum shook his head. Youth was damn well overrated. It seemed there was a whole lot to be said for older and more experienced women like Fay. He said, "It feels good. Hell, it's just skin. No cleaner or dirtier than any other skin." He held his hand in front of her face. "See that finger? Kiss it."

She did.

"Now suck on it and roll it around on your tongue like you did when you were a little kid sucking your thumb." She did that too.

"There you are," he said. "Same thing. Skin. But a finger doesn't feel as good to me and isn't quite as big to you. Now try it with that." He pointed.

"You're sure?"

"Hell, yes, I'm sure." He grinned at her. "You got a lot to learn, Cherry."

He laughed. "Soon as you learn this lesson, I'll teach you the next. First you pleasure me. Then I'll show you something that you won't hardly believe. You'll feel so good you might go outta your mind."

"Promise?"

"I promise."

"All right, then."

She bent over him and leaned close. He could feel her breath warm on the engorged, tight-stretched head of his pecker. "It doesn't smell bad," she said with a hint of surprise in her voice.

"Of course not."

Very tentatively she touched it with the tip of a cautious tongue. Then primly with her lips. "Gee, it doesn't taste bad either."

"Didn't I tell you it would be all right?"

"Yeah." She turned her head to give him a grin of sheer delight. Cherry Berry was previously uninformed, but she certainly was not unwilling. She acted as though she had just been give a new toy to play with. With a low squeal of enjoyment she took him into her mouth.

"Damn it! Careful of the teeth! Cover your teeth with your lips. That's better."

Slocum grinned as he continued to coach the girl. He supposed he should have told her, but he didn't feel like talking at the moment. And she would find out herself soon enough, anyway. After all, it wasn't as if she were a virgin or anything. By now she sure ought to know what happened when a man went over the edge.

Slocum felt the heat building and building, higher and hotter. He held it back as long as he could to increase the pleasure of the release, and when he finally came it was with a heel-pounding explosion of raw pleasure.

"Stay with it now, Cherry. That's it. Stay right with it." He held the back of her head and pumped what felt like a pint of steamy fluid.

She began to shake her head from side to side.

"Good. Real good, Cherry." He released her and she turned around. "You did real good, girl."

"I didn't know it was gonna do that."

Slocum laughed. "Well, you did all right, any-how, Next time you'll know an' be prepared better. The important thing is to stay with it till it's all over."

She sat up, wiped her mouth with the back of her hand, and licked her lips. "It doesn't taste bad. Just surprised me, you know?"

"You did fine. Next time you'll do even better."

She grinned.

"And I haven't forgotten my promise. Lie down. No, down that way. That's right. Now scoot up toward me a little. Fine. And spread. Let me in. Uh-huh."

At least the ignorant girl was clean about her person. Slocum applied himself to the business of the moment, and in less than thirty seconds Cherry was wiggling and writhing and starting to moan.

"Not so loud. We don't want to give your folks any ideas." That put a clamp on her mouth if not her feelings. She continued wriggling in silence.

Within minutes she wrenched her hips so violently that she bucked him off. She was quivering and shaking for long moments afterward.

"Golly, I didn't . . . I didn't *know!*"

"See?"

She reversed her position and rubbed herself all over him like a cat. "Thank you, thank you, thank you," she repeated, over and over again.

"Hey, no big deal, Cherry." Slocum was interested again. It was rather refreshing to be so well appreciated. He guided her back down where he wanted it. "Slip back down there and gobble on it a little more," he said, "just to get it ready again. Then we'll see what else you have to offer." He slid a hand between her thighs to the moist patch of curly red hair and beyond.

"Couldn't I do it French one more time? I want to see if you can do better this time. You know."

Slocum chuckled. "All right. Once more that way. Then I want to try you on for size."

"Just this once more. I promise."

Slocum lay back against his soogan and let the kid have her fun.

What the hell, he thought. Maybe there was something to be said for youthful enthusiasm after all.

Slocum rolled his bedroll and tied it behind the cantle of his saddle. He had a nice, empty, tender sensation south of his belt buckle when he went to bring the roan in and saddle it ready for travel. He tugged the cinches tight. A peaceful-thinking cowhand might have left that until the last moment, but Slocum had long ago learned caution. A man never knew when he might want to leave a place in a hurry, and he would inconvenience a whole herd of horses before he would take a chance on receiving a bullet in the gut.

With that out of the way he went to the seep to splash some refreshing water over his face. Only then did he turn toward the Berry wagon and the promise of a breakfast as lousy as the supper had been.

Still, there was some hope that it would not be so bad. It was Cherry and not her mother who was bending over the fire this morning. Of course the girl would have learned to cook from the old woman, but at least he could hope.

Slocum led his roan to the Berry camp and tied it to one of the remaining wagon wheels. He helped himself to a cup of coffee and was pleased to see that the brew seemed to be full strength. That was an improvement.

"Mornin'," he said.

Cherry gave him a smile. Her father grunted something that might have been a greeting. The old woman said nothing. Come to think it, Slocum realized, he had not yet heard Mrs. Berry speak. Likely she had nothing to say with a husband like that, he decided. He hunkered near the wagon and began to work on the coffee. The slab bacon and cornmeal mush the girl was cooking looked reasonably edible and he was willing to wait for it.

"Coffee," Chester said. He sounded grumpy.

"Yes, Pa." The girl interrupted her work to pour it for him and take it to him. She bent down to hand it to him.

"What's that in your hair, daughter?"

"What, Pa?"

"I asted what's in your hair, damn it."

"Nothing, Pa." She straightened and began to turn away.

"Damn you, don't you dare turn from me when I'm talking to you." He stood and grabbed her by the wrist, yanking her roughly back around to face him. "Turn your head now."

Chester pulled some dried grass stems and other small bits of debris from the girl's red hair, taking several strands of hair with it. "What the hell is this?"

Cherry shrugged. "Reckon I slid off the blankets last night, Pa."

"Huh. I seen you this morning 'fore you got up, and you was snugged down tight. So where'd this come from?"

The girl looked frightened. "No place, Pa. I mean . . . I don't know. It's nothing. Honest." She looked away from him and bit her lip.

She sure had a lot to learn. Slocum thought, in spite of all his work trying to teach her. If she'd looked the old bastard square in the eye and given him a halfway decent lie she could have gotten out of it clean.

As it was, Chester began to turn red with a flush of quick anger. "You been layin' on the ground, girl," he accused.

"I never," Cherry said, still without looking him in the eye.

"Damned if you ain't." Chester took a firmer hold on her wrist and yanked again, bringing her closer to him. "Harlot. You think I don't know what you been doing?" He turned toward Slocum. "Or with who?"

Slocum sighed, came to his feet, and turned to face the furious man. It seemed unlikely that a denial would be listened to. Besides, it was Chester Berry's problem, the way Slocum saw it. He hadn't raped Cherry, and a man can't be blamed for accepting an invitation.

"Bastard!" Berry screamed.

Slocum expected him to rush forward with his fists. Instead, Berry spun around and ran for the wagon box.

He grabbed a half-breed gun with a rusty barrel that looked like it was an old war surplus Springfield cut down and converted to a shotgun. Considering the type of slovenly bastard Chester Berry was, it was probably stuffed with nails and nuts and any other kind of scrap the silly fool could have found lying about. Whatever it was, Slocum had no particular desire to be shot full of it.

The roar and powder stink of a .45 Colt brought a halt to the developing proceedings.

"You might want to calm down now," Slocum said.

"Prick!"

"Only part o' me," Slocum said mildly. "Lay the gun back where you got it and step over that way. Unless you feel *real* lucky."

Berry swallowed hard several times, but apparently he did not feel lucky. He let the shotgun fall back into the wagon box and moved off in the direction he was told.

"A little farther," Slocum said. "That's better."

Cherry was crying. She covered her face with her hands and began making quite a production out of her sobbing. "He made me do it, Pa. He stuck his thing right in me. It hurt something awful, Pa."

Slocum grinned. Hell, he couldn't take offense. If the kid could get out of a thrashing that way, why the hell not. Anybody who wasn't willing to lie their way out of trouble was a damn fool.

"I'll get you, you bastard!" Berry shouted.

"Sure you will." Slocum removed the shotgun from the wagon, pointed it toward the sky, and touched it off. There was a hollow boom and a few wisps of smoke. Considering how long it would take Berry to reload, the weapon could hardly be considered a threat any longer. Slocum tossed it back onto the wagon floor. "Reckon I'll leave now, but I do thank you for the offer of breakfast."

"Bastard!"

Slocum grinned. "You sure have a lot to learn when it's the other fellow holding the gun, Chester."

With his left hand, he tipped his hat toward Cherry. He ignored her mother, who had neither moved nor spoken during all the commotion.

He untied the roan and turned it so he could step into the saddle without losing sight of Chester.

"Take care now, folks."

"You son of a bitch, you never showed me the way to that town," Berry yelled.

Slocum chuckled and touched the roan into a ground covering lope. He would have to stop along the way somewhere and make his own breakfast, but it didn't matter. His other appetites were pretty well taken care of for the moment.

5

Slocum stopped at the Picketwire to shave and bathe in the cold run of muddy water before he hit Trinidad and the dangers of recognition. Before him lay the abrupt rise toward Raton Pass; to the west the tips of the Spanish Peaks were visible. This was handsome country, low hills studded with cedar and juniper, the higher slopes forested and rocky. It had good grass too, whether high or low, and there was cactus, but not so much of it to be a bother. Slocum liked it. A few weeks ago he would not have been thinking in such terms. Fay waiting for him up ahead seemed to make a difference.

He worked up a lather from the dollop of soap he carried in an old snuff tin, sat down in the dark water to rinse, and could not help grinning with dismay at himself. He shook his head. John Slocum a damned goat farmer? Impossible. Or was it? It was tempting, he admitted to himself, more tempting than he would have thought.

Still, this was not the time to worry about it. He had made the woman a promise. There were damn few things a man like John Slocum might hold sacred, but his given word was chief among them. There would be time to think about other things when the promise was met.

He scraped his beard off with the blade of his knife. A barber's honed and stropped razor would have been much more comfortable, but the only barber surgeon he knew of hereabouts was up ahead in Trinidad. A visit to that chair hardly seemed advisable when there would be men in that town who could recognize him as a robber. So he completed the chore by feel with the keen edge of his belt knife and only winced a little bit from the tugs and nicks he could not avoid.

Finished, he let the afternoon sun dry his scarred, whalebone-hard body and dressed. He felt better when the Colt was once again buckled into place at his hip. He swung onto the tough roan horse and turned it upstream toward the town.

At the last moment, with the roofs of the town already in sight, he changed his mind. Discretion and good health were, after all, more important than a woman. He reined the roan south toward the higher hills.

If he wanted to get the views of men in this country who knew things that would not be known in town, the views of men who had heard the owl hoot and had ridden the lonesome trails, Dewey Cantrell's hog ranch was the place to do it.

Slocum knew of the place, but he had never been there. He had made it a point not to be seen there when he was planning the payroll robbery. You never knew who might be keeping an eye on a known hangout like that. Now it looked as though his past caution might pay off.

He guided the roan up a dim trail, angled up and over a ridgeline, and dropped down into a narrow basin beyond. As he had been told, Cantrell's place was half hidden in some firs at the head of the long basin. A running stream and beaver pond made a pretty sight below it. The creek and the boggy grass basin also gave a man the choice of coming and going without leaving tracks if he preferred. Slocum deliberately chose to ride in on the hard trail to eliminate suspicion if the wrong sort might be watching from some distant vantage point. There were probably a dozen horses already tied at the rails and not a single wagon. That alone was a tip-off about what kind of place Cantrell ran. Slocum tied his roan beside the others and went inside the long, low-roofed log building.

The murmur of conversation died momentarily when Slocum stepped through the beaded fly curtain covering the doorway. The men gathered at the plank bar and seated at the several tables paused in their talk to look at the man who had just joined them.

Slocum knew what they were seeing: a tall man, dark and lean, as tough as a rawhide reata and with a much-used Colt ready on his hip. His deep green eyes took in each of them as they assessed him. He was no pilgrim, and none of them was likely to be fool enough to try him. Not for sport. Not with his kind. One or two faces looked vaguely familiar, although he could not put names to them. He nodded toward those men and walked to the bar. The conversation resumed.

The man behind the bar was a large, competent-looking gent with sleeve garters, an oft-broken nose, and a walrus mustache.

"You'd be Cantrell?" Slocum asked.

"What's it to you?"

Slocum smiled, "You're Cantrell, all right. I've heard you're square. That's all."

Cantrell grunted.

Slocum pulled some silver from his pants pocket and laid it on the planking. "Bar whiskey. Whatever's cheap." There seemed no point in advertising the fact that he was flush. The less gold he showed, the less likely anyone was to connect him with the payroll job.

Cantrell grunted again and poured the requested drink. He selected coins totaling twenty-five cents from Slocum's change and left the rest where it was. Slocum nodded. In town a saloon of this quality would charge half that, but a hog ranch catering to the rougher trade could have gotten away with charging twice that much. It was the way he had heard: Cantrell was square.

"Something else?" Cantrell asked.

"Not at the moment." Slocum tasted the drink. It was neither better nor worse than he had expected. As raw and as rough as Cantrell's customers, but probably fit to drink. Safe to drink, anyway. Slocum savored the first fresh bite of the liquor on his tongue and let the rest of the shot slide down to warm his belly. Cantrell refilled the glass at Slocum's nod and took some more coins from the bar.

Another customer moved to the bar beside Slocum. He was, Slocum noticed, carrying a full glass. Not trying to put on the touch, anyway.

"Remember me?" the man asked.

Slocum looked him over. The man was wearing lace-up boots and a narrow-brimmed hat. He was one of the men who had looked familiar, but Slocum could not place him. Slocum shook his head.

"Dakota Territory. We played a few hands of poker."

Slocum gave him a thin smile. "Then I must've won that night. If you'd cleaned me, I'd remember."

"You won all right," the man said. "The gambler you was with did better."

It was Slocum's time to grunt noncommittally. He remembered the trip, but not the man.

"Join me for a drink?" The man grinned, pointing toward Slocum's glass. "We got a couple of bottles of bonded whiskey at the table."

"You talked me into it." Slocum downed his shot of bar whiskey and carried the empty glass to the table.

Two other men were seated there. Both were hard-looking men wearing shabby Stetsons, armed with revolvers and knives. The shorter of the two carried a Colt at his hip and a stubby bulldog revolver on his belly as well.

"Nate Smith," the one-time poker player said,

pointing toward the shorter and more dangerous-looking man, "and Jed. This here's John Slocum, late of Deadwood. I ast him to join us."

"You know him?" Nate asked.

"Well enough."

Neither of the other men offered to shake hands, but Jed shoved a chair away from the table with his booted foot. Slocum sat and poured a drink for himself. He tasted it. The poker player had been right. The contents of the bottle were a lot better than what came out of Dewey Cantrell's cask.

"Are you—uh—working, John?"

Slocum shrugged. "Loafing. Lookin' here and lookin' there. A man never knows what'll come along." He grimaced. "I hear this country's pretty clean at the moment. Hear they got a murderer all caught and ready to hang."

"That's the truth," the poker player said. "That the boy will hang, anyway. Not that he's a murderer."

Slocum's eyebrows went up and took another sip of the good whiskey, letting it lie on his tongue for a moment before he swallowed. "Kid named Bright, wasn't it? I don't think I've ever heard of him being in the—uh—business."

"You wouldn't," the poker player said, "because he ain't. He's just a nobody kid from noplace, unlucky enough to get caught in the middle of something he don't know anything about."

"But he'll hang, anyhow?" Slocum asked.

"Oh, he'll hang, all right. Law an' order will see to that. Even though. . ."

"You'd best shut up," Nate said softly.

"Huh?" The poker player peered across the table toward Smith and blinked. Slocum realized for the first time that the man must have been drinking for quite a while already. He held his liquor well enough, but there had been quite a bit of it, to judge from the slightly unfocused glaze in his eyes.

"I said . . ." Smith began.

"Aw—" the poker player waved Smith's suggestion aside—"you fuss too much, Nate. Fuck off." The poker player laughed.

Smith did not look particularly angry, but Slocum noticed his right hand moving slightly to scratch his stomach—just above the cracked gutta-percha butt of his belly gun. "I said you'd best shut up now," he repeated. "Matter of fact, you'd best leave now. Go get yourself some sleep or something."

The poker player laughed again. "You're a caution, Nate. Damned if you ain't. So calm down now while I catch up on ol' times with my friend John here."

"I *told* you . . ."

"Fuck off, Nate." The poker player turned toward Slocum and opened his mouth to say something.

Whatever it would have been, it never got said.

Slocum sat watching, quite ready if need be, while the man called Smith dragged his .455 bulldog from its pouch. If he had tried to point the gun toward Slocum he would have been a dead man. Instead he held it across the table, thumbed the hammer back, and shot point-blank into the poker player's stomach.

The gunshot brought instant silence into the saloon.

"What the hell, Nate?" the poker player gasped.

Smith shot him again.

The poker player tried to stand, tried to draw his own revolver. He was much too late. He toppled over and fell onto his side, his left leg kicking and jerking convulsively.

"Son of a bitch got abusive with me," Smith said into the silence of the long barroom. He looked toward Jed and Slocum for agreement.

"He cussed you," Slocum said, loud enough for the others to hear.

"It was justifiable as hell," Jed said quickly. "The way he was talking, I expected him to draw on ol' Nate here the very next thing."

Jed went on talking for a time, but Slocum was not paying any particular attention to him. His interest was in Smith's revolver and where the thing was pointing. It felt a little strange to find himself in the role of an innocent bystander. If Smith made the mistake of pointing the bulldog toward John Slocum, that role would change very quickly.

"That right, mister?" Dewey Cantrell asked.

"I reckon," Slocum said.

Cantrell nodded. The poker player was dying but not yet dead, and he was making quite a mess on the floor of the saloon. As gently as a man might want, Cantrell picked the gutshot man up and carried him away toward a back room out of sight. With luck, the poor bastard would die quickly. Without it, he would linger in agony for several more hours. What happened afterward was somebody else's business, but Slocum seriously doubted that the shooting would be reported to anyone.

He picked up his glass. The dying poker player's whiskey still tasted good.

Slocum eyed Nate Smith, who had returned to his seat at the small table.

Interesting, Slocum thought. The poker player—he did wish he could remember the poor bastard's name, assuming he had ever known it—had had a real definite opinion about William Bright's innocence and his coming hanging. He probably had been going to say more about that before Smith shot him.

Yet Slocum was not willing to say positively that Smith shot just because of that. The man hadn't looked all that upset, but then Slocum had known a good many men who would take fighting offense when some slob was stupid enough to tell them to fuck off. Nate Smith just might be another one in that category.

Still, it was interesting.

Slocum raised his glass toward Smith and downed the contents. Nate was not at all shaken by the incident, he noticed, and was calm enough when he picked up the bottle and refilled Slocum's glass.

"Long life," Slocum said as he tossed the next one down.

Smith and Jed grinned. "Long life."

From the back of the place they could hear a hoarse scream as the poker player went about the business of losing his.

6

Fay's nipples were hard, standing proudly upright. Her breath caught in her throat and she moaned softly as Slocum fingered the small, hard nubbin at the entrance to her hole. She reached between them and held him, her hand milling him in time to his finger flicks against that most sensitive bit of female flesh.

Her breath came harder and faster, and after little more than a moment Fay stiffened. Her back arched and her slim body shook and quivered in a spasm of quick pleasure.

"All done?" he asked teasingly.

Her answer was a groan of anguish at the thought of quitting so soon. She clutched him with both hands and pulled him to her, into her.

"Not done," he said.

"Damn you."

Slocum laughed. She pulled him deeper into her moist, ready flesh and pumped her hips beneath him, demanding to be taken, setting her own pace without his assistance. After a dozen strokes, Slocum gave up his pretense of disinterest and joined her.

He plunged into her again and again, the tempo of

their mating coming faster as the heat of their joining rose. Fay wrapped her legs around him, grabbed the cheeks of his ass in her strong hands, and hauled him deeper and faster into herself.

Slocum could feel her passion rising toward a second explosion, and the woman's freely given response sent his own pleasure soaring.

They bucked and humped with a furious intensity, belly slamming against belly, his balls swinging wildly to slap her ass, their sweat flowing and mingling.

Slocum felt the fierce heat explode, filling her with a long, fiery spurt of fluid. He drove himself all the deeper into her, trying to bury himself in her depths.

Distantly, very distantly, he could hear Fay's cries of pleasure as she joined him in release.

Exhausted, if only for the moment, he fell onto her and let the fullness of her breasts pillow him. She nuzzled into his neck with a slow sigh.

After a time—it seemed like a long while, though it could have been less—Slocum rolled off her and let himself sprawl beside her on the mattress ticking.

He raised himself on one elbow and grinned at her. "Reckon you haven't forgotten how, after all. Think we could say hello now?"

Fay chuckled. "Hello, John. Can I get you something. A cigar?"

"I wouldn't mind."

She left the bed and padded barefoot and naked the few paces necessary to cross her brother's small cabin. When she returned it was with an already lighted cigar, which she planted slightly off-center between his teeth. Slocum shifted the stogie to a more comfortable position and smiled at her.

"Did you have any trouble finding me?" she asked.

"Nope. Just stopped the first fella I came to and asked him where I could find the prettiest woman in town, an' the one likely to give the best time. He pointed me here on both counts."

"Is that supposed to be a compliment? If so, you have a lot to learn. I am the prettiest woman and give the best time in *Colorado*, not just in the town."

Slocum laughed and pulled her down onto the bed next to him. He wrapped an arm around her and let his hand find the weight of a full breast to play with while they talked.

Actually, not wanting to come face to face with any locals unless he had to, he had sat out under a stand of cottonwoods until he spotted Fay walking from the business district to the small cabin that had been her brother's.

Once he had the place spotted he waited until dusk and rode to it with no outward appearance of stealth. The surest way to call attention to yourself, he knew, was to look as if you were sneaking around. As it was, he did not think anyone had seen him ride in. But if anyone had they would not have seen anything suspicious.

He smiled. After all, a fellow wanting to pay a call on the newly arrived single lady would hardly be suspicious. Any man in his right mind would want to cut himself a piece of William Bright's big sister.

"What was that about?" she asked when she saw his smile.

"Nothing. A compliment . . . sort of."

She sniffed. "Maybe I'm better off not knowing, in that case."

"Probably," Slocum agreed. He drew on the cigar and was pleased to see that she had built the coal just fine. A many-talented woman, obviously. "How is it going here so far?"

Fay allowed her worry to show for the first time. "Not at all good, John."

"Have you found a lawyer?"

"One of the spineless pricks in this place? Hah! Not one of them."

"You turned them down or they turned you down?"

She sighed. "Oh, I asked, all right. Not counting the prosecutor, there are three of the pipsqueak bastards in this town. *Three* of them. Do you know what they told me?"

"I can guess, I think. But what was it?"

"They are all *so* busy. Just too busy to take William's case. Can you believe that? Can you?"

Slocum snorted. "I can believe they're scared to take it."

"Exactly," Fay said. "There isn't one of them with the first scrap of backbone to his name. They are all of them, every one, convinced that William is guilty. The whole town is convinced of it. And not a one of those lawyers is man enough to stand up to public opinion and try to defend him. Damn it, John, as far as these small-town bastards are concerned, they would rather see an innocent man hang than risk somebody's disapproval by defending his right to a fair trial. Why, that isn't . . . it isn't *American*."

Slocum gave her a sad smile. "But it sure is usual."

Fay snatched the partially smoked cigar away from him, dropped it into the empty tin can her brother had used as a bedside ashtray, and buried her worried face against his chest. "Hold me, John. Please."

He did, patting and stroking her for a time. When she seemed to feel calmer he held her away so he could look at her again and asked, "I guess you've talked to your brother, Fay. What does he say about the murder?"

She sat up and wiped her tears away with the back of her hand. "I talked to the sheriff first and then to William himself." She made a face. "They got a jail matron to search me before they would let me in to see him. It was embarrassing."

Slocum nodded. Fay Bright was not a particularly shy woman, but he could guess how humiliating the experience must have been for her.

"According to the sheriff, they have evidence against William which is more than solid enough for a conviction. The dead man and William had both been drinking in a saloon at the other end of town. The victim was a small-time rancher from northwest of here. He left first. William left the saloon right after him. There are witnesses—I don't know who they are or how many—who say William was muttering something and cursing when he left the saloon. The rancher's body was found the next morning in an alley about halfway between the saloon and William's cabin here. He had a knife still in his stomach, and he had been cut . . . well . . . to pieces was the way they put it. He had been cut up awfully bad."

"Stabbed or slashed?" Slocum asked.

She paused and looked confused for a moment. "Does it matter?"

"It might."

"I couldn't say for sure, John. I mean, that isn't something I would ask about. I got the impression from the way they spoke that the man had been slashed. One of them—it might have been the sheriff, or it could have been his deputy—said something about the rancher's throat and ears."

"Could you find out?"

"I . . . I suppose so. If it's important." She did not look eager to make any inquiries on that subject.

"It might be," Slocum said.

There was no point in raising false hopes with her at this moment, but a slasher who leaves his knife stuck in his victim's body would have to be a rarity indeed.

Slocum was no stranger to knife fighting, and he knew good and well that a blade once sunk into human flesh can be lodged so firmly that it would be impossible to pull it free without using another knife to cut it loose. On the other hand, a knife fight is normally conducted with slashes and slices against an opponent's flesh. A bone-deep stab *might* be the finishing blow. But if that were so, the attacker should have had the time to get his knife free afterward.

"Anyway," Fay continued, "the knife was left in the rancher's body. It was William's knife. A folding pocketknife, although bigger than most, I understand. The sheriff offered to let me see it, but I didn't want to."

Slocum nodded. To a woman one knife would be pretty much the same as any other.

"The sheriff said he has several witnesses who will testify that it is William's knife and that they have seen him use it any number of times. William told me himself that it really is his knife, but he doesn't know how it was used to kill that poor rancher.

"By the time I got in to see William I was pretty much upset, it's true, and mostly we spent our time hugging and crying. I . . . well, I didn't ask him very much about the murder. He told me that he hadn't done it. He said he remembers getting drunk that night and leaving to go home. He woke up when the sheriff and the deputy came to arrest him. He was sleeping right here in his own cabin when they came."

"What about the rancher?" Slocum asked. "Did he say anything about the rancher? About fighting with him, maybe, or being mad at him?"

Fay shook her head. "William said he had seen the man in town a time or two before and knew him to nod to, but as far as he can remember they had never spoken. Certainly he had no reason to kill the man.''

Slocum thought back to the evening before and the brief gunfight up at Dewey Cantrell's. A fellow could make a case for there being no reason for Nate Smith and that poker player to fight either, but the poker player was dead today, and he had had no quarrel with Smith before that.

"The witnesses said William was angry when he left the saloon, didn't they?" Slocum asked.

Fay said, "William remembers being annoyed because he ran out of money and wasn't ready to quit drinking for the night, but he doesn't remember being mad about anything. Certainly nothing to do with that rancher. I guess if he was muttering it was because the saloon wouldn't give him credit or something like that.''

At least, Slocum thought, Fay was not trying to color her brother as something he wasn't . . . like sober. The boy apparently had simply been too drunk to know what went on that night.

Too drunk to remember killing a man? Slocum wondered. It was entirely possible. It could well be that poor Fay was here on a mission of sentiment that had nothing to do with justice, just with an unwillingness to admit that her dear brother even when drunk could be capable of a grown man's heated anger.

"What do you think, John?"

"To tell you the truth, Fay, I think your brother needs

himself one damn fine lawyer.'' He was reminding himself that the poker player last night had been of the opinion that William Bright was an innocent man caught in someone else's crush. Slocum would never know for sure, not with the poor bastard dead and buried now, but the man might have had good reason for his opinion on Bright's innocence and his probable hanging.

''I know,'' Fay said, ''but there just isn't one to be had here in Trinidad. Not one who would even take the case, much less one William or I could trust.''

''Trinidad don't have any lock on lawyers,'' Slocum said. ''Denver's full of 'em. They're all a bunch of bloodsuckers, but some of them know their business. I expect I could come up with a name or two.''

That was a fact, he thought wryly to himself. A man in Slocum's trade tended to keep his ears open whenever a lawyer was spoken of as knowing what he was doing. It was a last resort, the sort of thing a man couldn't look to with any hope or certainty, but it never hurt to be cautious.

Come to think of it, though, he would have to caution Fay not to mention his name to any of them. Just as Slocum would tend to pay attention to lawyer's names, they were always on the lookout for possible clients. About any of the good ones should have heard of John Slocum. And Slocum did not particularly want Fay to hear about his background, especially not from someone else.

''I'll give you some names,'' he said, ''and some more money. A Denver lawyer won't come cheap.''

Nor, he was beginning to realize, would the cache of gold coins in his money belt last forever. At the rate this reasonably respectable way of living was eating up his funds, it was a caution how any poor devil ever managed to make it in the straight life.

"Tell you what else I'll give you," he said with a grin.

Fay squeezed him fondly. "I think I've already felt the idea that's come up."

"Good. I'd sure hate to surprise you with it."

She bent forward to kiss him, then continued her kissing in a line down across his chest and belly to the used but undefeated tool that was already rising and beginning to throb.

"Not bad," she mumbled. "Not *too* awfully small."

He laughed. Never had he been accused of being small.

The kisses turned to a series of slow, maddening licks.

"We only have until dawn," he said. "Then I got to get out of here or I'll compromise your reputation."

"Don't rush me," she said. "If you're here until daylight you just have to hide out inside the whole day long."

"In bed?" he asked.

She laughed and bent herself to the task again.

When he was ready, and far past ready, she straddled and mounted him, taking for herself the responsibility of pulling him into her and setting the pace of their stroking. She bent backward and reached under her slowly undulating rump to toy with his balls.

"Feel good?"

"Mmmm." Slocum grinned.

"I'm not so sure I like it when you grin like that," Fay said. "But I think maybe I do."

7

Jed smiled a hello and Nate Smith nodded, which Slocum figured was invitation enough. He was still curious about Smith and about whatever reason lay behind the poker player's death. He paid two dollars for a jug of the cheap whiskey and carried it to the table the two men were occupying.

"Mind if I join you?"

"Celebratin' something?" Smith asked with no particular welcome in his tone.

"Long life," Slocum said.

"Hell, Nate, he sided you the other night. The least thing you can do is invite the man to have a drink with us now." Jed grinned. "But next time, let us kick in on the price of the bottle. The bonded's better here."

"Sometimes a man can afford to be choosy and sometimes he can't." Slocum pulled out a chair and sat with them. He hoped Smith would not think of all the different ways that statement might be taken. On the other hand, Slocum did not really like Nate Smith a hell of a lot. Except for that question Slocum wanted answered, he would not at all mind if the man wanted to take offense.

Jed shoved his hand out to shake. "I didn't get a chance to talk much th' other night," he said, "but it's a real pleasure to meet you, Mr. Slocum."

"I don't have to be mistered, Jed." He filled all three glasses and took a swallow for himself. He had to admit that Jed was right about the quality of the whiskey.

"Yeah, well, it's a pleasure anyhow."

"What was it we were talking about the other night when that fella went and ruined the evening for himself?" Slocum asked of neither of them in particular. "Oh, yes—local law. Something about a kid bein' in jail down in Trinidad, as I recall." He tried to make it sound unimportant—just picking up the conversation after the poker player's rude interruption.

"Uh-huh," Jed said, obviously placing no significance in the talk. "Fella named Bright. Nothing much to it. He's gonna hang, that's all."

Slocum nodded and took another drink of the raw liquor.

Smith gave Slocum a look of speculation. "I never saw you around here before."

"No, I expect you haven't."

"I liked it that way," Smith went on nastily.

"Nate," Jed warned, "you'd best shut up."

"I never ast your advice," Nate said. He was speaking to his partner, but he did not let his eyes move away from Slocum.

"Nate . . ." Jed said in a low voice.

"Shut up, Jed. It's my own business if I decide I don't like *Mister* Slocum here. Come to think of it . . ." He reached forward with his left hand, picked up his glass of whiskey, and poured it onto the floor. "I don't think I want to drink his likker."

The cocky bastard's right hand, Slocum had long since noticed, was poised over the butt of the .455 bulldog revolver.

John Slocum had never been one to back down from a fight, not from any kind of challenge. He could feel the hairs on the back of his neck rise like the hackles on a feisty dog going stiff-legged with readiness when another cur came down the street. His jaw firmed and his eyes flashed green fire.

Under any other circumstances, Nate Smith would already be a dead man. But, damn it, he wanted to find out more about Smith and why he had killed the poker player. And, most of all, he wanted to find out what it was that the man from Dakota had known.

If Smith knew it too, and was covering it with that killing, Slocum wanted to share the knowledge. To do that, Nate Smith would have to remain alive.

The cold fire still flickering in his stare, Slocum grinned at Smith. "Kinda pushy for a man without braggin' rights, ain't you?"

"What?"

"What I said, Mr. Smith, was that you're a pushy little son of a bitch."

Nate's eyes narrowed. It was more than enough warning of what he had intended to do.

But this time, before his fingers could wrap around the butt of the revolver, Slocum's powerful fingers had clamped around Smith's wrist.

"Not that easy this time, Nate." Slocum grinned and backhanded him across the face, knocking Smith to the floor in a sprawling fall.

Slocum was on his feet and towering over Smith just as quickly. The instep of his boot jammed over Smith's wrist, pinning his gun hand to the sawdust floor.

"Not easy at all, actually." Slocum bent and plucked Smith's belly gun and then his Colt from their holsters. He tossed them aside. The guns skittered across the floor and thumped up against the bar, one of them hitting a makeshift spittoon and sloshing brown slop over the clean steel of the gun.

Slocum took Nate by the shirtfront and hauled him to his feet. He backhanded him a second time.

Smith had been shocked before by the suddenness of Slocum's attack. Now he was enraged.

He swept a roundhouse left toward Slocum's head, only to be greeted by a laugh as Slocum ducked easily under the blow and pummeled a quick left-right combination into Smith's gut.

Smith doubled over, his face going from rage red to ugly white as the breath was driven from his lungs.

Not wanting to miss out on the gift of opportunity, Slocum stepped lightly to the side and brought a boot up to smack Nate across the butt.

"Still think it's easy, Nate?" Slocum laughed and danced away from Smith's blind charge. He stuck a foot out and let the maddened Nate trip himself, to sprawl for a second time into the sawdust.

Smith crabbed around on all fours to face Slocum again, gathered himself, and launched himself toward the laughing Slocum.

Slocum set himself and would have turned Smith's face into a red pulp, but Jed leaped forward to intercept the man and pin Smith's arms to his sides. Jed was much larger than his partner, as tall as Slocum was and more heavily built, and he lifted Nate off the ground, unmindful of the man's struggles to break free and throw himself at Slocum once again.

"Calm down, Nate. Damn it, I said *quit*." He jerked his arms tight in a bear hug that sent the breath whooshing out of Nate's lungs for the second time in as many minutes. "Nate," he said calmly, "you got a suspicious nature, old pard. We got to have a talk, you and me." To Slocum he added, "Nate gets excited sometimes when he don't have to. I hope you'll understand that."

"He's still alive, isn't he?" Slocum returned.

Jed set Nate back onto his feet but kept a firm hold on one of his arms. "You oughta be grateful, Nate. Slocum's right. He coulda reamed your nose out with a .45 slug. I've heard that much and a helluva lot more about John Slocum, and believe me, you're one lucky bastard to still be alive. Now, the way I look at is this, Nate. Slocum was nice enough to offer you a drink an' you turned all nasty on him. I figure you owe the man an apology, an' we'll start all over." He looked toward Slocum. "If that's all right with you, that is."

Slocum forced a smile he really did not feel and

shrugged. "I just came in here to pass the time with a drink and a quiet evening. I reckon I'm willing to forget it."

"Nate?"

The smaller man grunted and grumbled, but after a moment he subsided. "All right."

Jed released his grip on Nate's arm. "All right, then. Step up an' shake hands like you ought to've done t' start with."

Smith shuffled his feet and swallowed hard, but after a moment he did what Jed told him. He shoved his hand forward and took a step without quite being able to look Slocum in the eye.

It was all Slocum could do was to keep from laughing. He felt at the moment like some kid caught in a scramble at recess, with the teacher making them shake hands and make up. He shook Nate's hand.

"Good," Jed said with enthusiasm. "Now sit down. Come on, both of you. Sit down." Jed busied about, setting the chairs upright, finding their glasses on the floor, and filling them from Slocum's jug. Most of the whiskey had spilled—small loss, Slocum thought—but there was enough to give them each a token snort.

After they had each had a short swallow, Jed sent Nate to buy another jug, this time a bottle of the bonded whiskey.

Nate seemed more or less mollified at the moment, but Slocum wondered how long it would take the man to remember that a room full of hardcases had just seen him whipped like a dog.

Still, the animosity had gone for a moment, and Jed seemed determined to make a good night of it. He told stories on himself—none, Slocum noticed, with Nate as the butt of the tale—and drew out of Slocum a few yarns about his own escapades. More, actually, than Slocum had intended to tell.

"See," Jed said at one point, "what'd I tell you, Nate? This ol' boy's been down the road an' acrost the valley. Bad as an old griz with a thorn in its paw when he wants to be. And he ain't woofing you, not hardly. Why, the things I've heard on John Slocum would curl the toes of the baddest bull in any patch of woods. He's took more money and lived to the far side of more gunfights than a Missoura whiskey maker." He looked at Slocum with admiration. "I swear, John, it's damn sure a privilege t' sit at the same table with you."

Jed took Nate by the arm and shook him a little. The smaller man seemed to be getting a bit bleary from all the liquor. "Hell, Nate, I got me an idea."

Nate blinked stupidly. "Huh?"

Jed laughed. "I reckon now is not the time to bring it up. You're too damn drunk to hear. Besides, this might not be the bes' place to discuss it. We'll talk about it tomorra, okay?"

Nate nodded, but Slocum doubted that he had understood half of what Jed said. His jaw was slack and his eyes were glassy.

"Tell you what, John," Jed said, "are you camped off in the hills someplace?"

Slocum nodded.

"I figured. So I tell you what." Jed burped. He was not immune to the effects of the liquor either, Slocum saw. "Tell you what. Me an' Nate, we got us a jim-dandy hole-up not half an hour from here. Plenty o' room. Extry bunks with good blankets. No louz . . . *lice!* . . . guaranteed. Not a one. Plenny of grub. No nosy bastards welcome. Don't hardly nobody know it but Nate an' me an' a few boys that are guaranteed all right, you know?"

Slocum nodded.

"So what I was thinkin' . . . maybe you'd like to ride along with us an' have a roof over yer head tonight." He belched again.

Slocum thought about it for a moment. He was not particularly high on the idea of bunking with Nate and Jed. But, with both of them well on toward being drunk, there was the chance he might learn something if he went along with Jed's invitation. He clapped the big man on the shoulder, picked up what was left of their bottle, and said, "When do we leave?"

Nate and Jed might have had some failings—a willingness to drink too much when there were strangers about among them—but poor judgment about horseflesh could not be included in any such list. Slocum would have been happy to fork either of the animals they crawled onto, and it was rare indeed for him to be able to make such a statement. Jed was riding a grulla with a chest like a barrel and a tough look in its eye, and Nate was mounted on a bay that showed an obvious infusion of hot thoroughbred blood.

Slocum suspected that either horse would be able to keep up with his own good roan to a day-long run. The discovery raised his opinion of the two and gave him a hint about their probable occupation as well.

Jed led the way, with Nate content to follow along behind his partner. That was just as well, because Slocum would not have consented to ride with Nate Smith at his back and he did not want another fuss with the man at the moment.

They rode east and south, winding into the mountainside away from the heavily traveled wagon road and rail line, farther and farther from Trinidad, into country Slocum had not covered before. The trail followed a ridge line to the south, but Jed turned off it on a slanting rock slab that would show no hoofprints and dropped into a stand of quakies before he left the rock for soil again.

Not bad, Slocum thought admiringly. They moved down into a draw, crossed the next ridge, and rode south into what looked like a boulder-stream dead end. From where they were now it appeared that there was nowhere farther they could go. Yet Jed had spoken of a cabin or at least some sort of substantial shelter at their destination. The man certainly acted as if he knew where he was going. Slocum pulled his roan to a slow walk, letting Jed and Nate get ahead of him while he studied the approach of their hideout. There might come a time when he would want to find it again.

There was a rock to one side shaped like a cat's head, and quakies to the other. A cliff off to the side had a tree—a juniper?—growing out of it. He was branding the details into his memory when a flurry of motion up ahead caught his eye and grabbed his attention.

Son of a bitch, he thought.

Four men—no, five—were rising up from the rocks with long guns in their hands. They were taking aim from cover, ready to cut down Jed and Nate, who still weren't expecting anything. They were damn fools to get so drunk they had lost their caution.

There was no time for a warning and no certainty Jed and Smith would react the right way if he did shout to them in time.

Slocum palmed his Colt and snapped a shot at the nearest of the ambushers.

The gunshot brought hell into play.

Jed and Nate snapped erect in their saddles and wheeled their horses aside without looking back to see what Slocum was shooting at.

Most likely, he realized, they would think he was shooting at their backs.

That impression was corrected by a fusillade of rifle shots from the startled ambushers who had expected an easy kill.

Lead spattered and whined off the rocks, but Jed and Nate were no longer riding where the ambushers had expected them to be, and the shots went wild.

The man Slocum had shot at seemed to be the only one in the bunch who realized that Jed and Nate were not alone. He turned and leveled his rifle at Slocum.

Slocum thumbed his Colt and fired again. This time his bullet knew the way. It thumped into the rifleman's chest and spilled him off his ambush perch to fall twenty feet or more into the gravel below.

He had no time to admire his handiwork. Slocum yanked the roan's jaw around and spurred it hard into the shelter of an aspen stand, bullets clipping the branches around his ears.

He kicked free of the saddle, pulling his Winchester from its boot as he dropped, and bellied through the tangle of young growth to the edge of the quakie stand where he could see what was going on.

It sounded like a war in progress a little bit up the draw. The rifleman was blasting away in the general area where Jed and Nate had disappeared.

One was fool enough to lean out from his overhead position to take aim on a rock where one of the men must have taken shelter. Whatever the reason, and whoever was in front of the rifle muzzle, the ambusher's movement put him in full view of Slocum.

Slocum took aim and squeezed off his shot with match-rest precision. The Winchester kicked back in recoil and a moment later the rocks beyond the rifleman were obscured by a fine red mist that sprayed from the far side of what had been a man's skull.

The blood must have reached another of the men, because within seconds Slocum could hear someone gagging and puking.

That, or simply the loss of two of their number, took the heart out of the ambushers. They began to scramble away.

Jed and Nate, sobered now, came out of hiding to speed the ambushers along with a drumroll of pistol shots. Smith, Slocum saw, was blazing away with both guns. It was impressive, except for the fact that he wasn't hitting anything.

No point in letting them have all the fun, Slocum thought. He peppered the ambushers' line of retreat with a few shots of his own. Not that there was anything in particular to shoot at. He could hear the men better than he could see them. All he could actually see was an occasional glimpse of a shoulder or a hat. But he wasn't going to be left out of it. He shot his Winchester empty, then palmed his Colt again, just in case he might need it.

He did not. Whoever the ambushers had been, they were long gone now. And there were not so many of them as there had been.

"Son of a bitch!" Jed yelled happily. "Lookit what you done, John!" He came down the draw at a run, a broad smile on his face. Nate trotted along behind him, looking a little green and the worse for wear, but definitely sober now.

"Hey, Nate," Jed called back to his friend. "What'd I tell you about ol' John here? Ain't you glad he come along?" Jed reached Slocum and began pumping his hand. "Saved our bacon is what you done, John. Damned if you didn't."

When he joined them, even Nate looked reasonably pleased to have had his life saved.

"What d'you say, Nate?" Jed asked.

"Well, shit," Nate said. "I expect I say thank you."

"You'd have done as much for me," Slocum said, knowing that it was a lie.

He felt like shaking his head, but he did not. Keeping this damn yahoo Nate Smith alive and available for conversation was looking to be maybe more trouble than it was worth.

Still, Jed seemed like a straight enough fellow, and he damn sure was grateful for Slocum's assistance.

"Come on, John. Hot damn, but we got a lot to celebrate tonight!"

Slocum reclaimed his roan and let the overjoyed Jed lead him the rest of the way to the hideout.

8

The hideout was ideally situated. Once they got past the bottleneck draw where the unsuccessful ambush had taken place, Jed led the way up a steep but negotiable chute into a hidden cirque with grass in the bottom and thick stands of aspen around three sides. A hand-dug well—there was no surface water to draw attention to the area—provided sweet water, and the log cabin had been tightly constructed by someone who knew his business. Judging from the age of the wood, Slocum doubted that Jed or Nate had done any of the work, but whoever had done it had known how to square his logs and cut tightly locking notches. The logs had been long weathered and were freshly chinked with mud.

"Nice," Slocum said. "But what about a repeat performance by your friends back there?"

"There's two other ways in or out," Jed said without concern. "Longer to get to the place that way, but there's not many that knows them."

"I thought practically nobody knew *that* way," Slocum said, hooking a thumb over his shoulder.

Jed grinned. "Practically nobody does."

"If you say so."

They unsaddled and turned the horses loose on hobbles to graze. There was, Slocum saw, a lean-to where livestock could get out of the weather, but there would be no practical way to pack hay in and there was not enough grass in the tiny bowl to be worth cutting for hay, even in the unlikely event that someone might be industrious enough to want to cut it. Night riders—and Slocum did not except himself in his assessment—were not known for seeking out hard labor.

"Nice," Slocum repeated when they entered the cabin. It was a well set up place with half a dozen bunks, plenty of fully stocked shelves along the walls, and a sheet-metal stove with a rack of split wood nearby. The center of the single room held a long table and stools, all handmade but apparently sturdy. It was the kind of place where a man on the run could winter without much worry, and Slocum tucked that thought away against possible future need.

"Throw your gear over there," Jed said. He pointed to an unused bunk. The only ones that seemed to be in use were two on the right, or west, wall. Slocum spread his bedroll and considered himself to be home—at least as much as he had been in many, many years.

Nate sat on his own bunk and kicked his boots off. He had not spoken for quite some time, Slocum noticed. He concentrated on rolling a smoke while Jed went about the routine chores of lighting lamps, starting a fire in the stove, and dragging a bottle of whiskey out of a wooden crate in a far corner.

"Come on, Nate," Jed said cheerfully. "We got some celebrating to do."

Smith joined them and accepted a glass of the liquor, but he drank little and spoke less. Slocum wished he could read the man's thoughts.

"Helluva nice job you did back there," Jed said. He grinned at his partner. "I told you, Nate, that John here was one curly-haired wolf from 'way back in the woods. Didn't I?"

"You told me, Jed."

"Damn right, I did, and he sure 'nough proved it. We owe you, John. Anything you want, you just name it, and it's yours."

Slocum was tempted to ask point-blank if they knew about the murder William Bright was accused of committing and how Fay's brother might prove himself innocent. If Smith had been as talkative and in as generous a mood as Jed, Slocum probably would have asked. As it was, he decided that caution was still in order.

"Your hospitality is plenty," he said to them.

"You got that, John. For as long as you're around here you got a place to stay, an' anything you find on the shelves you're welcome to. Food, ammunition, whatever."

Slocum thanked Jed.

"How long is that gonna be?" Nate asked.

"What?"

"How long do you figure to stay?"

Slocum shrugged. "Until I decide to move along, I reckon, whenever that is."

Nate gave him a look of skeptical inspection. "You here to do a job, maybe?"

"Damn, Nate," Jed protested. "That's not the sort of thing a man asks, an' you know it. I swear I don't know what's happened to your manners lately."

Slocum smiled at the nosy little bastard. "That's all right, Jed. It's one thing to ask. It's another to expect an answer. Isn't it, Nate?"

Smith glowered but said nothing.

"I tell you what," Slocum said, "for the moment let's just say that I'm resting and looking around. All right?"

"Hell, yes, it's all right, John. You don't owe us no explanations. No, sir. If anything, it's us that owes you. And, like I said—" he glared at his partner—"you're welcome here just as long as you want to stay. Come and go as you please an' no explanations needed. Right, Nate?"

Nate took a sip of whiskey, a very shallow sip which he took his time about swallowing.

"I said . . ."

"Right," Nate said quickly. "Long as you want, Slocum. No explanations."

Jed nodded, satisfied.

"I appreciate it, boys," Slocum said, choosing to ignore the minor tension that had risen between the two partners.

They drank for a time—or Jed did. Both Slocum and Nate were taking it easy with the liquor now.

They talked of inconsequential things; trails they had ridden, men they had known who were now in jail or dead.

"Same thing as far as I'm concerned. Except I reckon I'd rather go out clean than be caged for a life sentence," Slocum said.

For the first time Nate Smith seemed to be in complete agreement with Slocum. "Amen, brother. Amen to that," he said.

"Ah," Jed said with a negligent wave of his hand, "quit that kinda talk. Life's too damn short an' too damn much fun to worry over things that won't never happen." He was drinking directly from the mouth of the bottle now. He took a long pull, belched, and grinned.

"Maybe you're right, Jed," Slocum said with a smile.

"You bet I am. But listen, I been thinking. You, John . . ." He belched into his fist, gave the others a silly smile, and apologized. "What I been thinking, John, is that you're . . . uh . . . taking a rest right now. Figure you ain't real flush or you wouldn't be buying rotgut likker over to Dewey's place. Is that about right?"

Slocum shrugged.

"Well, what I was thinking, John . . ."

"Jed!" Nate said warningly.

"Now you hush, Nate. I got a right to say what I think, don't I?"

"Sometimes. I don't know as this is one of them."

"Well, I was just thinking that ol' John here . . .

an' you gotta admit yourself that he's a good old boy, saved our butts for us down there not two hours gone, you got to admit that.''

"I admit that," Nate said wearily.

"So what I was thinking, if John's looking for work, well, maybe we could find him some."

"I don't think you ought to get into that, Jed," Nate warned.

"Damn it, I think you're wrong. I think John'd be a real good addition."

"What kind of split are you talking about?" Slocum asked. "I wouldn't want to horn in anyhow if it's already a small take."

Jed waved his hand and took another drink. "It ain't like that, John." He grinned a trifle sloppily. "Regular wages, this is. *Good* wages."

Slocum shook his head. "I'm not much on hiring out for wages," he said. "I kinda like to get and go. You know how it is."

Jed looked genuinely disappointed, but Smith gave his partner a triumphant look. "See. I told you not to bring it up. He ain't interested. Now shut up, Jed."

Slocum would have been quite happy for Jed to rattle on. A man never knew when he might learn something if he just kept his mouth shut and his ears open. But this time Jed took Nate's advice, at least to the extent of changing the subject.

"It's gettin' on toward dark," he said. "Time we should think 'bout getting comfortable." He grinned.

"I thought we were comfortable already," Slocum said.

"Haw!" Jed guffawed loudly. "That's what you don't know. Ain't that right, Nate?"

This time Nate smiled too. "That's right, Jed."

"You want I should signal, Nate?"

"Go ahead."

With a sloppy grin, Jed left the table and wobbled his way to a shelf for a lantern. He lighted it with a straw he held in the stove for a moment and let the globe drop with a clatter. Jed giggled. "I'm ready, Nate."

"Go on, then."

"What's this all about?" Slocum asked.

"You'll see" was all either of the other two would tell him.

Out of curiosity, Slocum followed along when Jed lurched and lumbered drunkenly outside. Nate trailed behind. He was nowhere near being drunk now and Slocum suspected he just walked along because he wanted to keep an eye on Slocum, not let him have any time alone to question Jed with out Nate being there. That was indeed what Slocum had had in mind.

The three of them, with Jed in the lead, climbed the steeply sloping western side of the cirque to top out a hundred feet or so higher on a rocky, barren ridge line. Off to the west in the faint light of dusk Slocum could see a pinpoint of light not more than a mile distant, although separated from them by several draws and ridges.

"Neighbors?" Slocum asked.

Jed grinned at him. "The best kind." Neither he nor Nate would say anything more on the subject.

Jed scrambled to the top of a boulder, getting as much height as he could, and held the lantern aloft. He swung it back and forth with long, slow arm sweeps.

From acorss the distance Slocum could see after a moment an answering light as another lantern was swung from side to side over there. Jed was laughing with joy.

"What the hell?" Slocum asked.

"You'll see."

Jed held the lantern low, then raised it—once, twice, three times. He turned around, laughing again, and blew the light out.

"Now what happens?" Slocum asked.

"Now we go back down to the cabin," Nate said.

"That's all?"

"Wait an' see."

"I'm not a man that likes surprises," Slocum said.

"You'll like this one."

They picked their way carefully back down the hillside. The going was difficult now that the last of the light was fading from the western sky. Jed fell down several times. That worried Nate enough to take the lantern from his drunken partner, but not enough for Nate to help him. Back at the cabin Jed had himself a laughing fit, and even Nate was smiling a lot. Slocum wondered what the hell they could be up to.

Slocum heard them coming before they reached the cabin. High-pitched, chattering voices, laughing and calling out gaily.

Son of a bitch, Slocum thought. He looked at Nate. "Women? Way out *here*?"

"Jed told you this was a fine hole-up, didn't he?"

"I guess he did—but, damn! Women?"

Nate grinned. They had not been back in the cabin more than an hour. The visitors quite obviously came from the place several ridges west, and that was what all the signaling was about. The lantern had been raised three times, Slocum realized. Three lifts, signaling three men . . . or three women.

"Convenient," he said. "How many can you call up that way?"

Nate grinned. He was beginning to look excited too. "Up to five," he said. "The old fart's got five daughters. Hard up and too lazy to do much about it. Too scared to make an honest thief, so we help out. Keep him in whiskey an' a little eating money. When we signal he sends some o' the girls over. They like to have fun, so it works out for everybody."

Slocum shook his head with mingled disbelief and admiration. He had never heard of a hideout this well set up. Talk about easy living.

The girls came into view, entering the cabin without bothering to knock, and Slocum wondered if it was such easy living after all.

Well, he told himself, Smith had said the neighbor was an *old* fart. He would have to be somewhere in his nineties, if these were his daughters.

Slocum had gone and gotten himself all worked up for a romp with something along the lines of that

Cherry Berry he had run into. Now that one had been a girl!

He made a face, and didn't care a lick if they saw him or not.

The youngest of them was shading forty, he guessed. The others were already well into its shadow.

Drab was the best way to describe them—plain and drab. They might look better if there were a sack over their faces. They wore drab gray dresses which showed no shape at all, and had hard features with pinched-looking, thin lips and eyebrows woolly enough to make jim-dandy hairbrushes if they were whacked off intact. They had long, thin noses, wrinkles enough like furrows to plant a crop in, and plain brown hair done up in tight buns. They looked like a bunch of prissy schoolteachers. Slocum shook his head. He really didn't know how a man was expected to get it up if that was all that was available.

"Ma'am," he said politely to the nearest of them. He touched the brim of his hat. If nothing else, damn it, he still knew how to act proper.

The schoolmarish-looking spinster looked at him with utter surprise, threw back her head, and roared out her laughter.

"What the fuck is this?" she yelped. She marched forward and jammed her palm against Slocum's unsuspecting crotch. She turned and yelped again, this time with joy. "This un's mine," she cried.

That started a fuss with her sisters. They too insisted of feeling Slocum's tool, then began yelling at each other about which one of them should have him.

They were about to go to face-slapping when Slocum stopped them. He hollered, "Whoa, damn it!" That bought him a moment of silence.

"Don't I have something to say about this?" he demanded.

"Shit, no," he was told firmly.

Nate and Jed were about to piss, they were laughing so hard. "That's one of the rules, John," Jed bellowed between gulps of air. He was holding his sides and was in obvious, laughter-inflicted pain. "We just fuck whichever one crawls into bed with us."

Slocum shook his head, and the girls went back to their squabble, ignoring him for the moment. He left them, went to the table for a long pull on Jed's bottle, and then went to his bunk, where he sat and waited for the three look-alike sisters to work it out among themselves.

Eventually they settled it. How, he did not know or particularly care. They knotted up at the center of the room and went into a low-voiced conversation. When they broke apart, they all seemed satisfied.

Damned if they didn't still look like a bunch of prisses, Slocum thought, no matter how they were acting. He began to wonder if the whole thing was a put-on for Jed's and Nate's amusement.

One of them—he had not yet heard any names exchanged nor quite figured out any identifying features beyond old, older, and oldest—went primly around the room extinguishing the lamps until the place was in total darkness.

Next thing, Slocum decided, they'll all sneak out the front door, and I'll be left sitting here. He was convinced by now that it was all a bad joke with one John Slocum as its target. He was willing to bet money on it.

He heard the front door shut, cutting off the last hint of moonlight from outside. Uh-huh, he thought. All alone in the dark now. The girls have gone home.

A hand touched his leg.

As finely tuned as his senses were, Slocum had not heard or felt anyone approach. He damn near stuck whoever it was with his knife.

Then the hand went to his fly and began quite expertly to flick his buttons open.

A horrifying thought hit him, and he reached out to find a face to go along with that hand.

He felt relieved. The skin was not particularly soft, but there was no beard stubble either. Jokes—and more serious things—can be taken too far when you are among people you don't really know.

Whichever one she was, she did not say anything, but he could hear her laugh softly. It gave him no clue about which one had won him.

Deft fingers stripped his clothes away. A series of tugs and pushes directed his movements to accomodate the unseen hands.

He could feel her bending over him in the darkness, and he reached out to examine the body that was being offered—or that was taking something from him. He had not yet quite decided what was going on.

He found a slightly thick waist, traced the rib cage with his hands, and came to a smallish, definitely sagging tit. That was no clue either. He squeezed the tit, found the nipple, and pinched it. There was a sharp intake of breath, but he had no idea if it indicated pleasure or pain. She said nothing to let him know either way, so he did it again. and he felt his hand being removed from the tit.

She pushed him back flat against the bed and joined him there. The unseen woman's body was warm and dry against his skin.

For a moment he was afraid she wanted him to kiss her, and he did not want to do that, whichever of the three this was. Instead she busied herself with touching him, admiring the length of him, and holding his cock against her belly while she felt it and cradled his balls in one hand.

Slocum was surprised to discover just how worked up he had gotten from this. He was steel-hard and far past ready.

The woman chuckled in his ear and moved to receive him.

When he mounted her, she wrapped herself around him as if she was trying to envelope him. Her arms and legs clutched and pulled at him with a harshly demanding strength. She even tried to wrap her head around him, hooking her chin over his shoulder and clinging to him.

He was socketed deep inside her without consciously willing it to happen, and when he began to stroke into her, her response was as fiercely demanding as was her hold on him.

She humped and bucked under him with a furious energy that swept him up and over almost before he knew it was going to happen.

Hot fluids bathed her inside, and she only held him tighter when he collapsed on top of her.

She chuckled happily into his ear again.

They lay locked like that—Slocum still with no idea which woman's flesh was impaled on his massive tool—for several long minutes.

Then she began to move beneath him. He did not expect to be ready again so soon, but he was. He hardened and became rigid as the woman fucked him and then he joined her, once again ramming and driving with all his strength.

Her energy was incredible. She met his every thrust with a whimpered little grunt of extreme effort as she slammed herself upward against his belly.

When he came this time he could hear the tearing rasp of her pleasure forced from her throat.

Slocum was exhausted. He rolled off her, wanting only to rest for a moment. Later, he thought, he could explore other possibilities with whoever she was. Right now he only wanted to recuperate.

He breathed deeply and groped around on the floor for his clothes. He wanted a cigar while he rested.

He felt a shift of weight on the bunk, and the heat of her body was gone from beside him. Probably wanted to clean herself off, he thought contentedly.

He heard the front door open and saw a flicker of black against gray as a shadowy form left the cabin.

Slocum sat up. He stood and felt around in the darkness, but he was alone except for the sounds of breathing at the far end of the cabin.

A match flared down at that end of the cabin. Jed, naked, left his bunk to find a lamp and light it.

Slocum was amazed to discover that the three men were alone in the place. He had not heard the other two women leave, and wondered if the others might have waited and all left together. He shook his head.

Jed and Smith laughed. They must have understood his confusion.

"Which one . . ." he began.

Jed shook his head happily. "We never know neither." He laughed harder. "And don't care. Just be grateful, John. An' remember them lamp signals."

Slocum shook his head again. Son of a bitch. He found that desired cigar and lighted it. Not bad advice, he decided. Kind of like the mouths of gift horses. He helped himself to a swallow of bonded whiskey. Damned if he didn't feel pretty good now.

9

Even with a woman's homey touch, William Bright's cabin was a crude contrast with the spacious, orderly neatness of the outlaw hole-up high in the hills south of town. On the other hand, Fay Bright made for rather more enjoyable company than that provided by Jed and Nate Smith. Slocum hung his hat on a peg by the door and returned Fay's welcoming kiss with interest.

"Two days is a long time without you, lover," she said when she finally released him.

"Actually," Slocum said, "I was wondering if you'd still remember me." He pulled a cigar from his pocket and nipped the end from it. Fay struck a match and lighted it for him. He grinned at her. "Always did like a woman who knows her place." She jabbed him in the ribs and he grimaced. It hurt like hell.

"So much for servitude," he said.

"Servitude. Ha! One of these days we'll have the vote. Mark my words, cowboy. Then we'll show you a thing or two."

"Heaven forbid," Slocum said. He had to dodge

another sharp poke toward his midsection. He caught her and pulled her close, changing the subject.

When they broke apart again he said, "At least now I've figured out how to shut you up when I want to."

Fay gave him a superior smile and did not bother to answer.

She went to the stove to pour coffee for both of them and joined him at the small table. "So, John, what have you been able to accomplish?"

Slocum made a face. "Not a damn thing, far as I can tell. I listen a lot, but no one seems to be talking much about your brother's troubles." He did not want to go into it in any more detail than that.

"Can't you just—well—ask them?"

"Not in places I've been doing the listening. Good country for highwaymen and thieves up there toward the pass. They can pick and choose their victims along the road or any place in northern New Mexico or southern Colorado, hit where and what they want, and be across the borderline into another jurisdiction in a few hours or so. Real good country for them, and they have their own hangouts up there where they can be comfortable." He smiled. "When they ain't working."

"I don't think you should go there anymore, John. It sounds too dangerous."

Slocum choked back a laugh that threatened to spray her and half the room with a mouthful of coffee. Still Fay had no idea what kind of man he really was. She had no notion at all that the other men in Cantrell's or any similar saloon would be in more danger from him than he ever would from their kind.

"I'll be careful," he promised solemnly.

She looked only slightly mollified.

"What about you?" he asked. "Any luck down here?"

"A little," she said. "I did hire a lawyer."

"One of the ones I suggested?"

She nodded. "I. Thomas Hayes. What does the I stand for?"

"Hell, I don't know. Never thought about it. Old I-Tom is one hell of a lawyer, though. He can tie knots in the devil's tail an' use nothing but his tongue to do it."

"I certainly hope so. The man charges enough for his services. And he said he can't be here when the sheriff said they will go to trial. Mr. Hayes said he can get a delay, but the sheriff says he won't go along with that. I certainly hope it works out the way Mr. Hayes promised."

"What's I-Tom charging these days?" Slocum asked. When she told him he damn near choked. "You're joking."

"I wish I were. But it has to be done."

"You're still way short of that, aren't you?"

"We did not get onto this subject just so I could get more money from you, John. You've done more than enough already. Besides, I think if I sell the goats and my horse I can raise the money. I'll sell the homestead if I have to."

"Can't," Slocum said. "You haven't proved up on it yet."

"Well, then I'll . . . sell *some*thing. I can't let my brother hang because of a few dollars."

"Don't worry about it." Slocum dug under his shirt and pulled his money belt loose. "How short are you?"

"I can't, John."

"Hell, woman, it's *our* money, ain't it? Now, how much?"

Son of a bitch! Had he really said that? Of his own free will, and everything. He hadn't had any idea he was going to say it until it was out of his mouth.

That right there was more of a commitment than Slocum had thought he would ever make to a woman. And he had gone and done it without her having to say or do a thing.

There was something about this woman that was special. No getting around it. She just plain made him feel like an honest life was possible when he was with her. And he wanted to be with her more and more. The more time he spent with her the more time he *wanted* to spend.

Still thinking about that, he spilled the bright yellow coins out of his belt and realized with something of a shock that there was very little left over. His fat stake intended for some easy living was all of a sudden elsewhere.

No point in letting Fay know what he was thinking, though. He smiled and shoved the coins across the table to her. There were only a pair of the double eagles left. More than a month's pay for most men—if he wanted to look at it that way, which he did not—but damn little when he thought about what he had started with in that belt.

"John, I don't know how to repay you."

Slocum grinned at her. "I might have a few ideas on that subject."

Fay smiled. "Silly. You were going to get that anyway."

"I'd damn sure hope so. Come to think of it, what are we doing sitting here when we could just as easy be over on that bed getting all sweaty and wore out."

"My, don't you just talk sweet and turn a lady's head."

Slocum laid his cigar aside, and began shedding his clothing.

Fay was not far behind him. She stood slim and proud and naked before him, and he motioned for her to stay there for a moment so he could look at her.

She was a fine-looking woman. Quite aside from the fact that she pleased him just by being there, she was good to look at. He particularly enjoyed the sight and the feel of those magnificent breasts. She smiled and came to him, her breasts swaying with her motion.

"You're a helluva woman, Fay Bright."

She laughed and made a curtseying motion, even though she was wearing nothing but the patch of hair in her crotch. "Thank you, sir, say I. And you, I must say, are quite a man."

He never had a chance to respond. Fay pounced on him and knocked him backward, sprawling across the bed. Her fingers dug at his sides. As soon as she had concluded that he was not ticklish she began pinching and lightly biting him everywhere she could reach. The way she continued to swarm over him, she was able to reach an amazing number and range of places.

Slocum was laughing so hard he could not defend himself. "Quit, damn it, quit!" She kept right after him.

"If you don't quit . . ."

She assaulted him anew, her fingers and nipping teeth a blur of motion.

"All right, I warned you."

Slocum grabbed her and began to tickle her.

Fay began to squirm and try to get away. "Stop it."

"Ah, the worm turned, did it?" He tickled her some more. In less than a minute she was breathless and choking, subdued for the moment.

Slocum wound up lying half on top of her. Both of them were on the floor. He could not remember getting there.

"Uncle!" Fay cried.

"I ain't either. That'd be incest."

"Your intentions are carnal in nature, then?"

"Damn right they are." He proved it by hauling her the rest of the way around so they were lying mouth to crotch and planting a deliberately loud kiss into the curly patch of hair that was in front of his face.

"In that case," Fay said softly.

"In that case, what?"

"In that case, I'll join you." She took him into her mouth.

Eventually he had to plead that her attentions were becoming painful to an overused weapon.

"I always heard," Fay said, "that one lusty woman could outlast a dozen men. Now I believe it."

"The way I count it you still have eleven to go to prove that. You want me to go round up eleven men from the nearest saloon?"

"Don't try me, friend. Besides, you're as good as any other dozen men. I've already proven my point." She unwound herself from him and stood up. "Hungry?"

"As a bear in the first thaw. Trot it out and I'll eat it, whatever it is."

"Me?"

"If you can stand it, so can I, woman. Bring that thing over here."

She gave him a playful slap on the top of the head. "Not until you shave, you animal. I'm getting whisker burn so bad I'll hurt for a week every time I have to pee."

"It's your own fault." Slocum climbed to his feet and tried lighting the cigar again. This time he was able to smoke it. Fay was busy at the stove, slicing and frying.

"Aside from getting a lawyer," Slocum said, "have you learned anything interesting in town?"

Fay shrugged. Over her shoulder she said, "There is more talk about local politics than about William, damn them. Everyone is all excited and taking sides between two rich men who both want the same contract. Some sort of coal thing with the Denver and Rio Grande Railroad. I don't understand it all, but apparently the one who ends up with this contract will be in control and the other one will be pushed out. Very big locally. Personally, I wish . . . *ouch!*"

"What's the matter?"

"This grease is splattering." She turned around, wiping her stomach and breasts with a towel, and found an apron. She put that on and draped the towel over her chest before she went back to the frying pan.

"You were saying?"

"I was saying I wish they'd pay more attention to finding whoever the real murderer is than all this political nonsense. Ten seconds after William is out of jail, I'm going home where I belong." She stopped what she was doing, turned, and looked at Slocum. She looked . . . if not exactly wifely, wearing nothing but a short apron and a soiled towel, certainly domestic. "John. Will you . . . will you be going with me?"

Slocum smiled. Damn, but he liked this female person. He crossed the small room to take her into his arms and hold her.

"I reckon," he said, "that I'll give it a try. For a while, anyhow. Assuming the offer's still open."

Fay began to cry. She held him very tightly, smearing his back with grease from the spatula she was still holding.

Slocum figured that the offer was still open.

10

Slocum rode south into the hills and turned east. Dewey Cantrell's place was the best and the best known hangout for the rough crowd preying on the old Santa Fe Trail, but Jed had told him about another one in the dry hills to the east. Slocum headed that way after he left Fay just as dawn was breaking. He rode with the sun in his eyes and the brim of his hat pulled low.

It was a clear, fine morning, with no breeze, so sound carried for seemingly impossible distances. Slocum heard the high-pitched yapping from a den of coyote pups somewhere off to his left, the crash and crunch of a pair of does breaking cover from their cedar bed to his right. Somewhere ahead he heard a woman crying. His left fist rolled backward to tighten the pull of the reins and the roan came to a stop with its ears pitched forward. Colt in hand, Slocum eased the horse on up a sharp rise. When he topped it, he could see an interesting scene below.

There was a man, a girl struggling in the man's grip, a saddled horse, and a burro standing unattended nearby.

Interesting, Slocum thought.

He was not particularly high on the notion of rape, if only because he had no need for it when he wanted satisfaction. Besides, it annoyed the victim and showed bad manners on the man's part.

What really interested him, though, was that the son of a bitch who was so intent on putting it into the little Mexican girl, who looked to be no more than twelve or maybe thirteen, was one of the men who had been in those rocks at the entrance to Nate's and Jed's hole-up the other day. Slocum had very little use for people who shot at him.

With an evil grin on his face and green fire dancing coldly in his eyes, he kneed the roan and guided it down the slope toward the pair struggling below him.

The man had the kid's skirt torn off her, and she was wearing nothing else under it. Her skinny thighs were pale in the sunlight, and her hips were still those of a child, not yet swelled with approaching womanhood. The man ripped her loose blouse free, and Slocum could see that the girl's breasts were no more than buds, barely hinting at what they would become with time. She was crying and pleading with the man in Spanish, but the fellow did not seem inclined to listen.

Poor fella couldn't speak Mexican, Slocum thought charitably. His grin grew all the wider.

The man was a handsome, clean-cut-looking bastard, in spite of his current activities which showed that that ran no more than skin deep. He laughed and, keeping a hold on the girl's thin wrist, dropped his trousers.

Slocum chuckled deep in his throat; it sounded as much like a growl as an expression of amusement. That right there, he decided, had to be the source of the poor bastard's frustrations. He just wasn't hung very well. What there was of it, though, was standing tall, and the Mexican girl cried all the harder and closed her eyes at the sight.

Slocum thought about doing both of them a favor by shooting it off, but the way the girl was flopping at the end of the man's grip like a trout on stout line, he was afraid he would hit her instead.

"Good mornin'," Slocum said agreeably. He stopped the roan a few paces from them. "Getting a little morning exercise?"

Both man and girl froze in place. Only the man looked up at the lean, dark, dangerous figure sitting a horse above him. The girl slumped to her knees and seemed to give up. No doubt, Slocum figured, she thought he was just another damn gringo come to join in the sport.

"Who . . . ?" the man began.

"Oh, you oughta remember me," Slocum said. "We tried to shoot each other a couple of days back. Too bad I missed. But, hell, now I can correct the oversight."

Still grinning, he holstered his Colt and stepped off the roan on the right, keeping his eyes on the other man and not wanting to let anything get between them. Convention had it that a horse should always be mounted or dismounted from the left, but that was a convention begun by flatland cowboys. Anyone who rode in the mountains demanded a horse that was comfortable being used from the uphill side, whichever that might happen to be. And a man in Slocum's position could not afford to ride a horse that would be boogered by any damn thing, regardless of normal reasoning.

"You . . . ?"

"Uh-huh," Slocum agreed. "Me. Mind turning loose of the kid for a minute?"

The man glanced at the cowering girl. He looked startled, as if in the past few moments he had forgotten that he still had a grip on a naked twelve-year-old.

He looked sickly pale. He faced John Slocum; he faced death. He licked his lips and looked apologetic. "Look, man, I . . . you want her? I'll give her to you. She's prime." He released his grip on her and she dropped, exhausted, to the ground, doubled over with her knees to her flat chest, eyes closed and still crying. She was free, but apparently too frightened to think about trying to run away.

"Do you like to fish?" Slocum asked. His grin looked nastier than ever.

The man seemed surprised, unable to cope with the totally unexpected question. He swallowed hard and licked his dry lips again. After a moment he answered, "Not . . . not really." It was obvious from the sudden fear in his eyes that he desperately hoped that was the right answer.

"Something you learn when you fish," Slocum said, "is that it's a good idea to throw the little ones back. Let them grow to eatin' size and live to reproduce more of their kind."

"Really?" The fellow had not yet made any connection between that and what was going on here. After a moment he flushed. "Oh."

"Good," Slocum said. "Now, why don't you pull your pants up. You might catch your death standing there naked like that." He gave a slight emphasis to the word "death" and laughed. He could see the muscles in the scared rapist's ass tighten, and Slocum laughed again.

"Do it," Slocum ordered in a crisp, harsh voice.

"Yes, sir." The man bent and pulled up his trousers. He was very careful to keep his hands well away from the revolver which was holstered on his belt.

"You can pull that iron any time you want," Slocum said in a conversational tone.

The fellow shook his head violently from side to side. "I've heard about you," he said. "You'd kill me sure."

"I do expect to," Slocum agreed cheerfully.

"Not with no gun." The man used his left hand to unbuckle his belt again and pull the belt free. The holstered revolver fell to the ground untouched when the support of the belt was removed.

The man looked more comfortable now. He seemed to relax, sure that Slocum would not shoot him while he was unarmed.

"Silly bastard, ain't you?" Slocum said. He drew his Colt slowly, took his time about cocking and aiming it. He pointed it just left of center on the man's chest.

"You'll die too if you do," a voice came from Slocum's right.

A man was standing there. There was no sign of a horse, so he must have come up afoot when he saw what was happening. Slocum recognized him as another of the men who had participated in the ambush at the draw.

"Everybody is going to die," Slocum said. "The only question is when." He looked past the newly arrived man and laughed. "You, now—you're gonna die a whole hell of a lot sooner than you expect."

"If you think you're going to get me with that old one, you're out of your mind. The great John Slocum—and I'm gonna be the one known for killing him. No, don't let that pistol move the least bit toward me, or I pull this trigger."

He was holding a sawed-off double-barrel shotgun with both hammers back. It was hardly an idle threat.

Still, Slocum looked at him and laughed. "Yep," he said loudly, "a lot sooner than you figure to."

"Bullshit," the man said.

It was the last thing he ever said.

The sharp tines of a pitchfork skewered his neck, impaling him on manure-crusted steel, and an expression of stark amazement flickered in his eyes.

Slocum thought it rather interesting just how tough human hide is. As sharp as they were, the tine points stretched the skin forward for several inches before they broke through to allow the blood to flow.

Slocum looked beyond the ambusher to the squat, solidly built Mexican man who had slipped up behind while Slocum was talking. He gave the Mexican a wink, then returned his attention to the would-be rapist.

"Let's get back to the matter of what to do with you," Slocum said pleasantly. The flashing in his eyes said that the tone was a lie.

"You can't shoot me. I ain't armed," the man said. His voice was pleading, and tears appeared on his tanned cheeks.

"You know," Slocum said, "I've heard that same thing." He chuckled. "Never could quite figure out what kind of silly son of a bitch would believe it, though."

"Mister. *Please!*"

"You had your chance," Slocum said, "and you threw it away. Pity you won't be able to learn from your mistake. An' who knows, you might even have been able to outdraw me."

"I wouldn't've tried. I wouldn't . . ."

Slocum shot him in the chest, calmly recocked his Colt as if he were on a firing line, and triggered another slug into the man some inches below his belt.

Slocum turned to the Mexican man, who was rushing forward to grab the little girl and cover her nakedness with the rags that had been her clothing.

"Say," Slocum said, "I never thought to ask if you'd rather have done that yourself."

•   •   •

The girl's father was Obregon Carrera, a woodcutter and water hauler who lived in the hills southeast of Trinidad. Mindful of the dignity of gratitude, Slocum accepted his invitation to dinner and accompanied Carrera and the child to their home.

"Carmencita," Carrera said, smoothing the child's hair and wiping at the tear tracks on her face with a work-hardened thumb, "is the last of my little ones. She is the baby and the pet."

Slocum nodded his understanding. He was making the gesture of walking beside them and leading his roan along with their burro, and he was not especially comfortable on foot.

He could believe that the girl was the last of their brood, however many that might include. Carrera's thick hair was liberally sprinkled with silver through the black. The man's face was as dark as an Indian's and was seamed with deep wrinkles.

"I'm sorry this happened to her," Slocum said. "Hope she'll get over it."

Carrera sighed and held the child closer against him. "For a pretty child with brown skin, *señor,* it is a thing to be feared every day."

"With luck, maybe it won't happen again," Slocum said.

"Yes, *señor*. With luck." Carrera made the sign of the cross in the air.

They reached the jacal, a structure hardly worthy of being termed a shack, Señora Carrera and a whole herd of youngsters insisted that Slocum be treated as a hero after they first petted and washed the little girl and bundled her off inside the hovel.

They seated Slocum on a bench in the shade of an ancient cottonwood and waited on him hand and foot, pressing him with tortillas and steaming hot beans spiced with generous applications of jalapeno peppers.

Slocum filled up on the food and on the goat's milk they served with it. The milk tested a bit strange but, after all, it was time he developed a taste for the stuff. It was only good manners, he knew, to accept their offered hospitality fully. Besides, the beans were damn good.

"We know of no way to repay you for saving our Carmencita," Carrera said.

"You already have," Slocum said, wiping his mouth and belching with contentment. "That was a fine meal, ma'am." Señora Carrera, who did not speak much English but seemed to understand it to some extent, smiled happily and patted her own ample stomach.

Slocum stood and picked up his hat from the bench. He tugged it into place.

"If there is ever a thing we can do for you . . ." Carrera said.

"Don't worry about it," Slocum said. He looked around the swept earth yard in front of the jacal and saw only poverty there. The children—their parents too, for that matter—were barely clothed to the point of decency. There was no cash to spare in this home, and replacing Carmen's ruined garments would be a major problem for the family.

"Come to think of it," Slocum said, "there is one thing you could do for me."

"Name it, *señor*."

"Those tortillas your wife makes are awful good, and they'd carry well for a man riding. I wonder if I could buy some to take along."

"They are yours. Do not speak of buying, please."

Slocum shook his head. "No, I wouldn't feel right about taking them unless you'd let me pay. But I sure would appreciate it."

Carrera looked at him for a moment. Then he nodded and smiled. "As you wish, *señor*. It is not for us to deny you." He spoke to his wife in Spanish, and she hurried away to fix up a stack of the tortillas bundled in corn husks for carrying.

When she returned she gave the package to her husband, who in turn handed it to Slocum. He presented them with an oddly formal bow of his head. "With pleasure, *señor*."

"My pleasure," Slocum assured him. He gave Carrera a five-dollar half eagle for the dime's worth of tortillas. "If you think that will cover it."

Carrera looked at him, started to speak, but thought better of it. He cleared his throat and said, "Go with God, *señor*."

"I expect He knows me a whole lot better'n I know Him, but I'd appreciate any help you could give me in makin' an introduction."

"You are in our prayers, *señor*. This night and every other, from this day on."

"Reckon I couldn't ask for better," Slocum said.

He shook hands with Carrera and the oldest boys and mounted the roan, tucking his package of tortillas carefully into his saddlebags.

He felt a lot better when he rode away from the tiny jacal—much more so than a bellyful of good food might account for.

11

"What the hell is that I smell?" Jed's grin grew wider when he saw the slab of fried meat Slocum had on his plate.

"Help yourself," Slocum said. He pointed toward the haunch of fresh meat from the buck he had brought down on his way back to the cabin from a fruitless trip to the other owl-hoot saloon.

"Tortillas too. Where'd you get them?"

Slocum shrugged and cut himself another piece of the meat.

"Slocum?" Nate was standing in front of him.

"Yeah?"

"Maybe . . . well, maybe I been wrong about you."

"Because I brought in some deer meat? Seems hardly enough to get excited about, Nate."

"You know what I'm talkin' about."

"As a matter of fact, I don't." He sopped some juice up with a wad of cold tortilla and shoved it into his mouth.

"We heard about Lonnie an' Asa," Smith said.

"And who would those two gents be?"

125

"The two you gunned today."

"Oh." He burped. "Actually, I only shot one of them. Obregon Carrera spitted the other with a pitchfork. I don't rightly know which of them was which, if it makes any difference."

"It don't," Nate said, "but I still want you to know that I think I was wrong about you."

"That's fair enough, Nate."

Jed was grinning. "I sure am glad to see you boys getting along now. Damn! That's the way it should've been right along."

Slocum changed the subject. "Cut yourselves some steaks there, boys. The fire ought to be good and hot yet. I'd have waited for you, but I didn't know when you'd be back—or if you would, for that matter."

Jed nodded. "Don't wait for us tomorrow night either. We figure to be late then."

"All right."

"Nate?" Jed asked.

Nate nodded. "Go ahead, Jed. I guess you ought to ask him."

"'Bout what?" Slocum asked.

"About tomorrow," Jed said. "We have a job coming up. Thought you might like to ride along and pick up some extry money."

Slocum smiled. "I didn't exactly know there was such a thing as extra money."

"You know what I mean. Not bad pay, John. Forty dollars for a night's work. It wouldn't be anything you couldn't handle."

"Straight pay, not a split. That's not exactly my style, Jed."

"Well, it ain't the kind of thing where there'd be anything to split, you see. But it's easy work. Riding with a bunch of pretty good boys. I know they'd be real proud to have you along with us."

Slocum looked at Nate.

"I say it too, Slocum. You'd be real welcome."

"That's nice of both of you, but riding with a crowd for regular wages . . . well, that just isn't the way I do, boys. I hope there's no hard feelings about it, but I'd rather pass."

"All right. For sure there's no bad feelings about it. If you happen to change your mind, just let us know."

He nodded and went back to his meal. "Say, I couldn't find any coffee, or there'd be some ready for you."

"Right here." Jed showed him and took it out to begin making a pot. "Say, after supper you will celebrate with us, won't you?"

"That I can handle," Slocum said with a smile.

After they had eaten, Jed and Nate opened a fresh bottle and the three of them worked on it quietly.

"Hope you don't mind, Slocum," Nate said, "but we won't be swinging the lantern tonight. That sort of activity tends to sap a man's strength, if you know what I mean."

"I don't mind," he assured them.

He didn't, either. There were no promises between him and Fay Bright, nothing that would bind him or tie him down, nor were there likely to be any. But, for the time being, he was just plain thinking about her and the plans she had made for the future, plans that included him now.

He still could hardly believe that he had gone and said he would try his hand as a *nester,* of all things, a goat rancher. Goat farmer? Rancher sounded better, anyway. He could call it that if he damn well pleased, and pity the dumb bastard who might insist otherwise.

Maybe the time had come when he was willing to try a settled life in one spot for a while. But he was not going to cut his balls off and bury them in a piece of dry homestead land. No sir! He would walk as tall as a damn goat rancher as most men could thinking they were in the free and easy times. Anybody who thought different would get shown, but *proper*.

Just as soon as this business with Fay's brother was settled and done with, he would go make a try at it and see what happened. Hell, it couldn't be too bad, could it? He would file on the land and move in with Fay. Let her keep him drained. If that wasn't enough, he was making no promises—not to her, and particularly not to himself. He would just give it a try. If it worked out, that would be all right. If it didn't, he could walk away any time he wanted. No obligations. No ties. Nothing to hold him there a minute longer than he wanted to be there.

Sure, he decided. That was a good way to have it. A man could live with that.

He helped Smith and Jed kill their bottle and start on another. Finally they doused the lamps and went to bed.

• • •

The sound of blowing horses brought Slocum out of bed with his Colt in hand.

"Ease off, John. It's just our boys," Nate said.

Slocum nodded, but he kept the .45 ready until Nate went to the door and could see that the riders were the men he had been expecting. Only when Nate threw the door open and invited them in did Slocum holster his gun.

He dressed quickly and had his gun belt in place by the time the riders tied their horses and came inside.

There were six of them. Quite a crowd, Slocum thought, with Jed and Nate included. And they could have used another rider or gun as well. He wondered idly where they were going and what they might be up to. Not that he really cared; he was just a mite curious.

Smith seemed to be the leader or foreman of the bunch. It was obvious that Nate Smith was not the brains and money behind whatever they were doing.

Jed made introductions all around. Most of them were men Slocum had never heard of, although several of them acted as if they thought themselves pretty tough.

Local talent, he thought: plenty of brag and bluster. He would reserve judgement about how much grit they really had until they were tested.

It's one thing to make a reputation by running roughshod over a bunch of farmers and scared little town clerks. It's another to earn that same reputation by facing men with genuine sand in their craws.

The only one of the bunch Slocum had ever heard of was Perry Newcombe, a thin kid who looked to be no more than nineteen, if he was that old. The name rang a bell, and Slocum tried to remember where he had heard it.

He thought about it for a moment, and it came to him. Newcombe had been having some saloon refreshment down in Fort Stockton when some drunk sergeants tried to hoorah him. The way the story went, Newcombe had taken them all before they could get their service revolvers out of all the leather the brassbound military insisted on. He had killed one and put lead into the other two, then made a hard run south for the border. But apparently chilis and beans had not agreed with him as a permanent way of life.

The kid was the quietest of Smith's whole crowd. There was no brag about him, which Slocum did not find particularly surprising. He spoke with a British accent and looked as if he didn't even shave yet. Slocum made a point of shaking the boy's hand and speaking to him by name. The rest of them he really did not give a shit about; they were the kind he would have regarded as cannon fodder in an earlier day and time.

Jed got the fire going and Slocum helped out by reducing the rest of the venison haunch to crudely hacked steaks. Not pretty, the way a butcher would do it, but just as tasty. It was Perry Newcombe, he noticed, who picked up a bucket without waiting to be asked and went out to get water for the coffee pot.

Nice kid, Slocum thought. He wished the boy well.

They ate, and the bustle and chatter of so many people in the cabin, the loud jokes and the nervous laughter, reminded Slocum even more of the years he had spent wearing a gray uniform, learning to accept the idea of sudden death as any man's escape from life. The atmosphere in this hole-up cabin was very much the same as in the army. Only Jed and Nate and the Newcombe boy seemed little affected by it. They, at least, seemed to accept the coming night as a job of work that needed to be done.

When they were done, Jed and Perry Newcombe cleaned up. Had he been a part of it, Slocum would have stepped in to do it himself. As it was, he sat on his bunk and had a cigar. When they were ready to ride he wished them well.

"We'll be back some time tomorra," Jed told him.

"I'll put a pot on first light," Slocum said, "unless I decide to lay out somewhere else."

"Use the lantern if you want." Nate laughed. "With only one here, I reckon you'd at least find out which one you was bellied up to, for a change."

"If I'm here, I reckon I will." Slocum waved them goodbye and went to saddle his roan. After a night spent alone, he thought a visit to William Bright's cabin might not be a bad notion.

He let Smith's crowd get well clear and past any

point of ambush that might have been set up for them. Then he followed along behind at a walk. They were friendly enough, but it wouldn't be sensible to give them the idea that he was trailing them, particularly when he had no interest whatsoever in where they might be going.

He reached Trinidad before noon and thought about holing up until dusk, but hell, that would be a long time. He waited until there was no one moving on the street toward town from the cabin and rode in as if he belonged there.

"John!" Fay looked delighted. "What a wonderful surprise."

Slocum shut the door behind him and dropped the bar into place. He took his hat off and accepted the wet kisses she tried to cover him with. "What are you doing here?"

"I got this yen for a good fuck," he said. "Are you busy, or should I go up town to the cathouse?"

Fay laughed. She had been in the middle of preparing herself some lunch, but she ignored that now and began immediately to shed her clothes.

"Reluctant wench, ain't you?"

"It's not your body I care about, you idiot. I just don't want you wasting money when I can put those dollars to better use back home."

"I figured it was something like that." He stripped and joined her on the bed.

She kissed him thoroughly, her body warm and inviting against his. When she finally pulled back away from the kiss, she looked at him and smiled. "Hi."

"Hello yourself, woman."

"Just wanted to get laid, did you?"

Slocum smiled. "Something like that."

"How do you want it, big boy?" She threw herself onto her back and scissored her legs wide in a parody of a willing whore. "Plain old on and off?"

She jacknifed her slim body abruptly, spun, and flung herself down onto Slocum's stomach. "Or is it a French lesson you're craving? I'm good at that one, big boy."

She gave him a loud, lip-smacking kiss on the head of his cock and turned to wink at him and bat her eyelashes.

Slocum shook his head and laughed. It was no wonder he liked this woman, he thought. She was just plain fun to bed.

"Laughter? Is that it, cowboy? I offer you the best ass you'll ever have and you *laugh* at me? So much for you!" She climbed off the bed and stood with her back to him, hands on hips, nose high in the air.

Slocum grabbed her and pulled her back down beside him. She pretended to struggle for a few seconds, then broke up and came giggling into his arms.

"That," he said, "is better."

She kissed him and said, "You never did tell me which way you wanted it."

"Mmmm . . . how's about one of each."

"If you think he's up to it, cowboy, then I guess

I'm game too.'' She reached between them to fondle his tool affectionately. "I sure do like this thing of ours," she said.

"Ours?"

"All right, then. Mine." She bent and took him into her mouth, running her tongue around and around the sensitve head while she used her fingers to caress his balls.

"That one first, huh?"

She emptied her mouth to speak by applying hard suction and then pulling back against it. When he popped loose there was a loud, wet noise. "I would suggest this one first, then the drab old ordinary method. After that—" she gave him a bawdy wink— "we'll have to see."

"There's nothin' worse than a bossy female," Slocum said.

"You can always take that walk up the street," Fay said, "if you think you can find something better up there."

12

Slocum felt pretty good. He was freshly shaved and smelled of the bay rum Fay had given him as a present. His belly was full from the meal she had prepared, and his loins were thoroughly drained, also courtesy of the thoughtful Fay. A man would have to go some to be better set up, Slocum thought.

He fished in his pockets for a cigar and made a mental note reminding himself to buy some more the first chance he got. It was too late now or he would have sent Fay for some. At this hour, though, the only places that would be open would be the saloons and the whorehouses, and he could not send her to either of those. He thought about going himself. Clean-shaven as he was, there was little danger of being recognized.

Still, little chance was not the same as no chance. Those odds were not quite good enough, and he could wait. Cantrell should have something on hand, and Slocum had long since learned not to be choosy about brands or labels when there were risks that should be considered first.

Fay bent over to light the stogie for him. She had

gotten dressed a little while earlier to go fetch in some water, but even so she made a mouth-watering sight with that impressive bosom dangling in front of his eyes. He was thinking about trying to get it up just one more time when they heard the commotion down the street.

"That doesn't sound like anyone celebrating," Slocum said, rising to his feet.

Men were shouting hoarsely, and somewhere a bell was ringing. A fire bell? Slocum wondered. He looked out of the small window set into the front wall, but he could see no glare of flame over the dark, sleepy town.

"Lots of people are in the street," he said. Fay joined him at the window.

"That looks like the sheriff on the horse," she said. "There must be some kind of trouble."

"I'd like to hear what it is," Slocum said.

"It could have something to do with William."

"I don't want to hurt your reputation by being seen on the street with you. Better if we go separately," Slocum told her.

She looked as though she might have argued with him, but she did not want to spend the time that would take. Since she was already dressed, Fay gave him a quick kiss and hurried out. Slocum pulled his clothes on, strapped his gun belt in place, and followed moments later.

"What is it?" Slocum asked of a stranger in the street as he approached the crowd. The light, he was pleased to see, was very poor. There were no street lamps. A man wearing a badge, probably a deputy, was holding a lantern so the growing crowd could see the sheriff, who was still on horseback and sat well above the eye level of the standing people. A few others had thought to carry lamps or lanterns out with them, but the street was mostly in shadow.

The man Slocum had spoken to shook his head. "Damned if I know, but he sure wants everybody out."

Slocum stood listening with the rest. He noticed a good many women on the fringes of the crowd, but he did not see Fay among them.

"Boys," the sheriff said, "Jerry Rait just rode in with some bad news. There's been a raid tonight on the Cooper ranch. Most of you knew Coop. He's been a friend to us all. Now he's dead. The raiders shot him down when he tried to defend his home place. They fired his barn and shot him down when he came out with a gun in his hands."

There was a low, growling murmur from the crowd. Whoever Cooper had been, he seemed to have been well liked.

"Who done it, Tom?" someone shouted.

"We don't know that yet," the sheriff said, standing in his stirrups to look out over the crowd. "But we figure to find out. There must have been a bunch of them. They'll have left tracks. I want to get a posse together." He held his hands up and shouted, "Whoa! Don't start rushing off already. Hear me out first. We got plenty of time to do this right. There won't be tracking light till dawn, so let's get together and do this the right way.''

"Damn it, Tom, if we wait that long they'll have got clean away,'' another voice protested.

The sheriff shaded his eyes from the glare of the lanterns and peered across the half-seen faces that were turned toward him. "Is that you, Randy?"

"Ayuh."

"Do you know who they were?"

"Hell, no."

"Do you know where they went?"

"Nope."

"Neither do I," the sheriff said. "That means we got to wait until daylight to get after them. We got no choice about it, like it or not. I don't like it any more'n you do, Randy, but, like I said, we're going to do this *right*." He received a muttering, grudging rumble of assent from the angry men who had gathered.

"Now what we're going to do," the sheriff went on, "we're *all* going to ride together tonight. We go out to the Cooper ranch and we lay out a ways so we don't go milling around and ruining the tracks we got to follow come morning. All of us. Nobody out on his own. I don't want no false tracks to confuse me come daylight. You got that?"

Slocum saw a fair amount of nodding from the crowd, although none of them seemed pleased by the prospect.

He realized they all wanted blood, and they wanted it now. In a way, he found it interesting to be looking at a posse from this point of view. He more commonly saw them from a distance and it was usually his dust they were chasing, his tracks they were trying to pick up. Here, forming up, they were on the verge of becoming a mob.

"Right," the sheriff said. "Now, before we go to get our horses and gear together, I want those of you as is coming with me to step over here where I can have a word with you about what to bring and what you're going to damn well leave behind, lest I charge some of you with obstructing justice."

The men in the crowd moved to the side where the sheriff was pointing, shuffling forward nearly to the man. They left behind only some youngsters, one very elderly man, and John Slocum.

The boys were grinning and excited. Several of them tried to join the men but were sent rudely back. The old man spat and complained loudly about not being able to ride any longer.

Slocum looked up to find the sheriff staring at him. "Something wrong with you, mister?"

Son of a bitch. If there was anything Slocum did not need or want, it was to be spotlighted in the attention of the townspeople. Had he realized that in time, he would have stepped over into the posse group immediately. Hell, no one said he would actually have to show up to ride with them afterward. But he had not thought and now it was too late.

"Nope," he said.

The sheriff made a sour face. It was obvious what he was thinking, and Slocum reddened. Cowardice was not something he was accustomed to being accused of.

But if he stayed where he was and talked them down, the odds got longer and longer that someone was going to recognize him from that robbery, beard or no beard. A little fur on a man's chin, or the loss of it, doesn't change him all that much. He turned and would have walked away and to hell with what any of these rubes might think, but a new voice stopped him.

"I know that man, Sheriff."

Slocum froze in place, his blood running cold and his heart leaping to his throat in a lump that would have been impossible to swallow. If one of them had indeed recognized him, he would play hell trying to shoot his way out of a mob that size. Nearly every man in Trinidad was there, was armed, and was already on the fight because of their friend's murder.

He turned to face them, his hand curled and ready to sweep the heavy .45 into action.

"That's the man, Sheriff," the voice repeated. "He's the bastard that wouldn't help me out on the prairie, an' tried to take advantage of my little girl besides."

Slocum was confused for a moment. He had been ready to sell his life dearly for being recognized as a robber. Now it was almost with relief that he recognized Chester Berry as the speaker.

"Tried to abuse my baby, he did," Berry was saying, "and refused to give a stranded traveler help. That's the kind of miserable bastard he is, sheriff."

"Mr. Berry," Slocum drawled, "you really ought to be careful what you say about a man. There's some as don't like to be lied about, and I reckon I'm one of them."

Inside, Slocum was burning, a slow, ugly burn. What he wanted to do was force that miserable little prick Berry's hand and give him the bullet in the gut he so richly deserved. But, if he did that he would call just so much more attention on himself.

If they held some sort of inquest or hearing afterward, there would be no way he could count on poor light to protect him against recognition. For the moment he had to swallow it and let the little fool be.

But it gnawed at his gut even as he flipped the man a finger and turned to stalk away into the welcome darkness of the night.

Behind him, he knew, there were now several dozen men who would be thinking him a coward or worse.

That hurt bad.

Slocum had done a lot of things in his time. He had never done anything that would destroy his pride. Walking away from an ugly, lying son of a bitch like Chester Berry came damn close to it.

He could hear the crowd complaining behind him as he entered the circle of darkness around the lantern bearers. Those low voices made him feel as if he were slinking away like some skulking coyote.

Damn it, he thought with fury, John Slocum goes like a wolf, not like a coyote.

But he was going, just the same.

He tried to shut his ears to the men, but he could not. He could still hear Berry's whining, complaining, lying voice until he was far down the street toward William Bright's cabin.

Even then he found himself lurking in the shadows like some kind of coward.

Oh, he had a perfectly good reason. He did not want anyone to think ill of Fay because of his presence in the cabin she was occupying.

But knowing he had a valid reason did nothing to make him feel any the less a slinking coyote of the type he despised. His head told him that he was right, but his gut told him he was wrong.

He worked his hands into fists and imagined the sweet feel of Chester Berry's throat in his hands, the satisfaction he would have if only he could feel his Colt buck and roar and send a pellet of hot lead into Berry's stomach.

But he did nothing except stand and wait in the shadows until he was sure he would not be seen entering Fay's cabin.

John Slocum felt lower than at any time he could remember.

"Why so glum, John?" Fay touched his face with gentle fingers, but Slocum could only turn his head away from her. "Is it because of what that man said out there?"

There was no point in wishing Fay had not heard. She had been there, standing with the other women, and she had heard every bit of it.

"I know it couldn't be true, John. If you are worried that I might believe it . . ."

He pulled away from her with a curse and sat angrily at the table, wanting to hit someone—anyone— wanting to fight and punch and kill anyone except Fay. She had not earned his anger, had done nothing to deserve punishment. If he took his feelings out on her it would be totally unfair, but he wanted to vent his anger on someone.

"Please, John."

"Please what?"

"Please know that I don't believe any of that nonsense."

"Those men out there do. That sheriff does. Some of them are good men, too. The sheriff is. Not everyone would have bothered to send you a wire about your brother, you know. A man like me—well, even I have to respect someone like that."

Fay followed him, stepped into his arms, and made it clear that she wanted to be held. "To begin with, John, Sheriff Tom Atkins didn't send me the telegram. The town marshal did that. Rolfe Kuner is a nice, thoughtful man, and I would feel better about William if the case was in his jurisdiction, but it isn't. I don't trust Sheriff Atkins at all. He's an oily talker, and I don't believe a word he says. Certainly I couldn't care a fig what he thinks about you or anything else."

Atkins. The name struck a chord somewhere in Slocum's memory, although he did not think it had anything to do with law enforcement.

"Secondly, John Slocum, I won't hear any more talk about what kind of a man you are. I *know* what kind of man you are: the very best kind. You don't have anything to be ashamed of. When I needed your help you didn't hesitate. You were there for me. That's what I know about you, John. You are a fine man. Don't you ever let anyone tell you different. And don't *you* ever try to tell *me* different."

Slocum felt miserable. He had this good and decent woman believing in him. That, if anything, made the night's events all the worse.

He had not only been humiliated in front of a crowd of rubes, he was being made to feel that he had deliberately deceived the only person he had cared about in he could not even remember how long. He did not want to think back that far.

"Fay," he said hoarsely, "it's time you and me had a talk." He sighed. "You might want to withdraw that offer you made me a while back."

"I won't. I can promise you that, John."

"No, I reckon you can't, not until you've heard what I have to say."

She smiled trustingly up at him. "Whatever it is, John, I care about you. It won't change anything, I promi—" He held a finger over her lips to quiet her.

"Not until I've told you what kind of man your 'cowboy' really is." He led her to the table and sat her down.

"Listen to me now. Then you can change your mind. I won't blame you, not the least lick. That I can promise you, Fay. I wouldn't blame you at all."

He sat across from her, his face pained. He pulled out a cigar and lighted it for himself. He took a deep breath. Then he began to speak. He talked for a long time, late into the night, there was very, very little that he did not tell Fay Bright.

And if, come morning, Fay decided that in good conscience she had to turn him in to the law, that would be her right. He would not hold that against her, either. That was a promise he made to her right at the beginning, without saying it aloud. It was a promise he intended to keep, come what might.

13

Slocum could hardly believe how damned good he felt, or how fortunate he was.

Fay Bright was as good a woman as any ever could be. Even knowing what she did about him, she was sticking with him. She had been angry with him for doubting that she might. Now that, he thought, was a woman.

He nudged the roan into a lope and grinned into the crisp morning air. The sun was barely up but he was already halfway back to Nate's and Jed's hole-up. He had left Fay's cabin long before first light to make damn sure no one saw him leaving. That woman deserved better than for him to give her a poor reputation. And if there was anything he could do to help her, he would surely do it.

Before, he had just been hanging around, not really taking that big an interest in her brother's problems. Now, if it would please Fay for him to accomplish something, that was what he intended to do. He owed her. He wanted to repay her.

He stopped at Cantrell's to buy cigars and a couple of bottles of whiskey. His money was running low but, what the hell, there was always a way to pick up a little more. Dewey's face was red-eyed and puffy, and Slocum got the impression that the man's sleep had been interrupted. For a celebration? Probably. It would have been poor form to have asked. Besides, Slocum figured he could guess the answer without bothering to ask.

He rode on to the cabin, finding fresh tracks of horses entering the cirque and leaving it again. Nate's bunch, he figured.

As he had expected, only Jed's and Nate's horses were there when he arrived. Both had been hobbled and turned loose on the limited graze in the bowl. Slocum pulled his saddle, hobbled the roan, and turned it out with the others.

"Mornin'," he said. He deposited his whiskey bottles on the long table and tossed his saddlebags, freshly loaded with smokes, on his bunk.

Jed and Smith were in bed. They sat up and looked at him owlishly, blinking the sleep out of their eyes. Jed threw a balled-up sock at him and grumbled something about "noisy bastard," but he was grinning.

"Everyone came away clean, I take it," Slocum said. He filled the coffee pot with water from the bucket, started a fire, and set the pot on the stove.

"Slick as a whore's snatch on a Saturday night," Jed said.

"Good." Slocum added chunks of wood to the kindling he had started and hunkered in front of the firebox to make sure the wood caught. "You caused quite a stir in town last night," he said.

"Yeah?" Jed was chuckling. "Tell me about it."

Slocum told him. Nate was awake and listening, but said nothing.

"They should've been tracking for a couple hours now," Slocum concluded.

Jed laughed. "For all the good it'll do."

"If you're sure none of your boys got careless, it won't do them any good," Slocum agreed.

"Single file all the way," Jed said cheerfully, "an' no one set a foot anyplace that Nate didn't want 'em to go. He's a smart fella, this partner of mine."

"Good enough," Slocum said. He grinned. "Reckon I can rest easy, then, and let this coffee finish cooking. Otherwise, I might be tempted to slide on out of here."

"There's nothin' to worry about with Nate in charge," Jed assured him.

Slocum nodded. Smith seemed not to have heard the praise; at least he did not react to it.

"You're awful quiet this morning, Nate," Slocum said.

"I keep thinking about something."

"Yeah?"

"I keep thinking that you know who we all are an' where we been. That worries me, Slocum."

"Aw, come on, Nate. John saved our butts when those boys came at us that time. And he shot Lonnie and Asa, didn't he? Hell, he's square."

Slocum shrugged. "I can see your problem, Nate, but there's only two ways you can go from here. One is to let it be. The other would be for you and me to have it out. If that's what you want, we might as well do it here and now."

Slocum stood and faced Smith. Nate's revolver was hanging by his head beside his bunk. If he wanted to reach for it, that would be his decision— and his tough luck.

"Don't . . ." Jed's voice trailed away. He waited to see what his partner would decide.

Smith scowled. He sat up in his bunk, looked at Slocum and at the revolver. It was temptingly close to his hand. He looked back toward Slocum. There was a calm certainty about Slocum, a casual, almost uncaring attitude.

Nate smiled. "We'll just forget I said anything, Slocum."

"Right." Slocum was not smiling. They might forget Nate had said anything, but Slocum did not intend to forget that Nate had thought about it.

"All *right*," Jed said happily, quite obviously willing to forget the whole thing. He stood and stretched, pulled his clothes on, and came to the table to wait for the coffee to finish brewing.

Nate dressed and set about making breakfast for all three. Slocum noticed that Smith left his revolver hanging holstered where it was. He stayed well away from the gun while they ate, and afterward he sat with Slocum and Jed at the table over extra cups of coffee.

"Yeah," Jed mentioned, "it all went slick as grease last night, with old Nate here in charge. Couldn't've been better."

"That rancher didn't hurt anybody?" Slocum asked.

"Naw. Never come close. We had a couple boys waiting outside the door, off to the side where he wouldn't see. The rest of us was whooping it up around the barn, raising the old Ned and making noise. Cooper came out an', *blam,* they cut him down 'fore he knew they was there."

"Slick," Slocum said.

Interesting too, he thought. So it wasn't just a raid to burn a barn as they thought in town. They laid for Cooper and just used the barn fire to draw him out into the open.

That was interesting—and just as interesting was the fact that Nate Smith was sitting there without a word of protest while his happy, talkative partner told Slocum all about it.

Nate had made it pretty clear time and time again that he was a closemouthed fellow. It seemed out of character for him now to listen and sip coffee and not appear to give a damn while Jed talked.

Slocum grinned. Hell, if Smith was determined to take it that way, this might be a good time for Slocum to ask some questions. He wasn't likely to get a better chance, and Jed was a trusting soul. He wouldn't think a thing about a good friend like John Slocum being interested in the way Jed and his smart partner did things.

"This Cooper," Slocum said, "he stepped on some toes, did he?"

"Yeah," Jed said. He reached for a biscuit and began smearing jam on it. "You could say that.

Took up land where a certain party we work for needs to be.''

"How's that?" Slocum asked. Still no response from Smith.

"Me and Nate—you too, if you want to come in with us—work for a fella who's in a fight for a coal contract. The Denver and Rio Grande needs coal. They use a lot of it, and down here they really burn it. Getting over Raton Pass takes a lot of engines, they tell me. Not that I know anything about that, but it's what they say.''

Slocum nodded. It made sense. The wonder was that they could build a grade through the pass at all. Dragging a loaded freight up it would require awesome amounts of raw power.

"Anyway," Jed went on around a mouthful of biscuit, "whoever gets the contract for the coal is gonna be a rich man. He'll have all the say-so around here. The loser will be on the outs. Might as well pack up and go somewhere else.''

Again Slocum nodded. It was a common enough situation. You would hardly ever find two men who were willing to share a fat prize—not when one of them could get it for himself without a split.

"The fella we're working for is supposed to be the loser. That's the way most of the betting is going. There's a few in town who're in the know, and they'll ride right along with him on the upswing when he comes through with that contract.''

"So what does some rancher way the hell out of town have to do with it?" Slocum asked.

"Simple," Jed said. "Cooper was sitting on a rich deposit of coal. If our boss can show the railroad he has these big reserves all sewed up, he's sure to get the contract, 'cause the railroad just has to have that coal. What we're doing is kinda helping him to get the reserves. And when the dust clears, John, it's gonna be good around here for all of us that've been with him. That's why I say you oughta come in with us. It could really set you up. I mean really."

"Was this Cooper the only one sitting on the reserves your man needs?"

"Naw, but he was the biggest one left. Some of them sold out. I mean, it ain't like the boss is greedy, you understand. He made each an' every one of them fair offers for their ground. And, hell, grass grows just about anyplace. They could've moved along with cash money in their pockets. We only have to deal with the ones that've gotten stubborn and unreasonable."

"It sounds pretty good," Slocum said.

"Then you'll come in with us, John? Damn, I hope you will. We'd sure be proud to have you. Wouldn't we, Nate?"

Smith gave Slocum a thin-lipped smile. "You bet," he said.

Slocum did not believe him for a minute. He would have believed Nate fussing at Jed to keep his mouth shut, or Nate strapping on his gun from force of habit and the hell with what Slocum might think about it. But this was a bit much for Slocum to accept.

"I appreciate it," Slocum said, "but, like I told

you before, I'm kind of set in my ways. I like to score and move on. See some more country and have me some fresh women. Staying in one spot just ain't the way I like to do things.''

"I was afraid you'd say that, John. But, if you change your mind, we'd still be glad to have you in," Jed said.

Slocum stood and yawned. "I think what I'm gonna do is ride over to Cantrell's and see if I can pick up a line on something a lone man could do to make some money."

He saddled and rode, and the farther he went the stranger he thought Nate Smith's responses had been.

Just for the hell of it, Slocum decided, it might not be a bad idea to turn off, away from this trail he was taking. He turned the roan south, upslope toward the ridge lines above the usual trail to Cantrell's.

It rarely hurt to be a little cautious. Better foolish and alive ten times than bold and gutshot just once.

14

Slocum pulled the roan to a halt, stepped down from the saddle, and tied the horse to a stunty cedar. He pulled his Winchester from the boot and eased on foot to the other side of the ridge, where he could get a better look at the slope. He smiled to himself.

No, he thought, it never hurt to be careful.

And unless the deer up here had taken to wearing hats, that was a man lying up in the rocks above the trail he was looking down on.

The man shifted position slightly. Bored? Slocum wondered. Impatient for a target he knew was coming? Slocum could see the glint of sunlight on steel and the checkered pattern of the man's shirt.

Careful to make no noise on the loose rocks underfoot, Slocum eased down above the waiting man. He moved slowly, taking time and care. Quiet was much more important than speed now.

He smiled as he came closer. What a surprise, he thought. He moved to within a few paces of the gunman, slipping silently down from an unexpected direction with his Winchester held loosely now in his left hand.

"Howdy, Nate. Fancy finding you here." Slocum was grinning.

Smith spun, his jaw slack with surprise. "What—?"

"What am I doing here? I was just about to ask you the same thing. You—uh—left Jed to home?"

Smith's eyes hardened and he stood, leaving his rifle where it was on the boulder behind which he had been crouched. This was belly-gun range, anyway.

"I don't trust you, Slocum, and never have. Poor Jed, he trusts most everybody. It's one of his faults."

"Uh-huh." Slocum smiled. "The truth is, Nate, I'm not in any position to criticize. I guess I haven't learned to trust *you* a hell of a lot either. Otherwise, I'd likely be dead by now."

"You still will be," Smith said.

"You got to prove it, Nate. You can't just talk me to death."

"Oh, I can prove it, all right. I . . ."

Smith's hand flashed. He clawed for the .45 on his hip, and he was fast.

But not fast enough.

Slocum's Colt bellowed, and Nate took the slug high in his left hip. The impact of the bullet spun him half around.

With Smith's right side toward him, Slocum shot into it. The bullet hit Nate in the arm and passed through into his ribs. His unfired revolver fell to the ground as his arm went numb.

Slocum had to give him credit for being game. He staggered, but he managed to turn to face Slocum again.

He tried to find the butt of his .45 belly gun with his left hand, but Smith's limbs no longer seemed to be following instructions. He fumbled at the gun, but he could not find the strength to grasp it.

His knees buckled and he fell forward to topple face down on the hard ground.

"I expect you did find out, Nate," Slocum said.

He went forward quickly to turn Smith over. He took the belly gun from its holster and threw it over the boulder toward the trail below. He found Smith's Colt on the ground and threw that over too.

"You killed me," Smith said.

"Could be," Slocum agreed. "We'll know in a while."

"I'm shot bad."

"I've seen men die from less," Slocum said cheerfully. "On t'other hand, I've seen them live after worse."

"I don't want to die," Nate said.

"Not a whole lot do," Slocum said.

"Get me to a doctor, man."

Slocum shook his head. "I can't think of a single good reason why I should, Nate. Hell, I went to a lot of trouble to put those bullets into you. Why should I help you get them out?"

"I know . . . I know what you want."

"Really?" Slocum rolled his eyes skyward and mused for a moment. "Let's see. Wealth. Everybody wants that. Easy livin'. I expect we all want that too. What else, Nate? What is it that I want so bad I'd help you just so I could get it? And you a man who has tried to kill me."

"That woman," Smith said. "Bright's sister, she is. I seen you going into her place."

"Really?"

"Yesterday. Yesterday it was. I had to go into town on the way to Cooper's ranch. Had to talk to the boss. I seen you go into that cabin."

"So?"

"So you was asking questions about Bright when you first showed up here. It's him that brought you here. Him and that big-titted woman."

Slocum gave the man a wry smile and shook his head. "You know, Nate, for a man who wants help, you sure are willing to flap your jaws in ways that annoy a fella. That big-titted woman is *my* woman, and I don't really like you talking about her that way."

"I'm sorry. Godamighty, I didn't mean it like that." Sweat was beginning to break out across Smith's forehead. The shock was beginning to lessen, leaving room for the pain to come in.

"Hurting, Nate? Just give it another couple hours and you'll be screaming your throat raw and begging somebody to kill you just to stop the pain." Slocum smiled at him. "You've seen it happen before. Probably done it yourself to more than a few. Haven't you?"

Smith gritted his teeth and nodded. He was sweating freely now. "You got to help me, John."

Slocum laughed.

"No. I can help you, Slocum. I swear I can. You and that woman of yours. Just get me to a doctor. I'll help you. *I don't want to die."* He was close to panic now.

"I can't see it, Nate."

"Damn it, man, *I'm the one that killed the rancher your girl friend's brother is fixing to hang for."* Smith was clutching his hip with his one good hand. Bright runnels of scarlet blood seeped from between his fingers. He began to weep, the hot tears rolling down his cheeks.

"I tell you, Nate, that does not really surprise me a whole hell of a lot. But I don't see that knowing it is worth carrying you to a doctor. You know an' I know that you can just shut your mouth once you get there, and there wouldn't be a thing I could do about it."

"My God, man, have some mercy."

Slocum shook his head. "Fresh out, Nate."

"Look. I'll make a deal with you. I'll make the confession. I swear I will. If . . . if I don't, Slocum, you could kill me after. I know you could. I've heard what kind you are. You wouldn't give a shit if the governor was watching. If you had a reason, you'd shoot first and then worry about getting away. I know that. Take me in and I swear I'll tell the sheriff who done the killing. I swear I'll get your woman's brother out of jail. *Give me a chance, Slocum."*

Slocum pondered it for a moment. He shook his head. "Easier to let you die, Nate. I can always spring the kid from jail, if it comes to that."

"Slocum, I *swear* to you . . ."

"Aw, I don't know, Nate. Of course, you're right about one thing. I could always kill you later." He smiled down at the hurting man. "You do know that I'd do it, don't you, Nate?"

"I know. I know you would." Smith reached up and tried to clutch at Slocum's sleeve.

"Don't do that, Nate. Your hand's all bloody, and I don't want to have to wash this shirt again." Slocum looked at him. Smith was in agony now. "All right, Nate. But I expect you'd best make your confession before I let a doctor tend you."

"Anything. Anything, John. I swear it. I wouldn't try to cross you. I swear it."

"Sure," Slocum said. He went to bring his horse down and to find Smith's.

Sheriff Tom Atkins looked tired. His eyes were red-rimmed from fatigue. He probably had spent the night and most of the day in the saddle, and he looked it. He also looked surprised when Slocum carried Nate Smith into his office and laid the wounded man across the top of the desk.

"This man has something to tell you," Slocum said.

Atkins came to his feet. "I better get the doctor right away."

Slocum took him by the arm. "In a minute, Sheriff. First hear what he has to say. Then go get the doc. Otherwise—well, I made the man a promise. I figure to keep it." He looked down at Smith and winked. Smith would know as well as he did that while the sheriff was off finding a doctor, Slocum would have more than enough time to finish Nate Smith. And he would damn sure do it. Slocum had worked that out and discussed it with Smith at some length on the ride to town.

Smith fought back a wave of pain and got the words out that meant the difference between certain death and possible life.

"Sheriff, I . . . I'm the one that knifed and killed John Trent. Bright didn't have nothing to do with it. I found him passed out drunk, so I lifted his knife and used it to kill Trent. Left it in the body to cover my own tracks. Now . . . please get me help. I'm shot bad. I'm scared I'm dying, Sheriff."

Atkins nodded and hurried out.

"I got to admit it, Nate," Slocum said. "You surprised me. I kinda had you figured to try something funny at the last minute, but you took your medicine like a man."

"Get out of here, you bastard. Leave me be. I did what you wanted. Now leave."

Slocum stood. He thought about doing exactly what Smith asked. After all, Slocum had already had entirely too much attention from Sheriff Tom Atkins as it was. He could get along nicely without any more.

Something seemed a little . . . *off*. Slocum was not entirely sure just what it was, but there was something. Enough, whatever it was, to curb his inclinations to get out of the sheriff's sight and keep him there.

There had been Nate Smith's unprotesting confession, for one thing. A promise, after all, only goes so far. Faced with a probable hanging if he confessed, Slocum was almost sure that Smith would recant at the last moment and refuse to make his statement before the sheriff.

And, too, Slocum now realized, there had been no surprise in Sheriff Tom Atkins's expression when Nate made his confession. In fact, the man had scarcely paid attention to it.

Most lawmen Slocum had known—and there had been altogether too many of them over the years—would have been far more interested in getting the confession than the doctor. Atkins had paid scant attention to the words, and had run immediately for medical help.

Odd, Slocum thought. He grinned, then laughed out loud. "You know, Nate, I have to give you credit. You know your business better than I thought you did."

Worry joined the pain in Smith's expression. "What's that supposed to mean?"

"It means you almost got away with it, that's what. But I think I know a way to fix it now."

"Damn it, Slocum, I did exactly what you wanted, exactly what you told me to do. Now get out of here and leave me to die in peace."

Slocum laughed. "You may die after all, Nate,

quicker than you think.'' He turned and hurried out the door.

There were few men on the streets of Trinidad: a horseman riding past, a few loafers sitting in front of a mercantile. Slocum called to them, asked them to hurry into the sheriff's office to witness an important statement. The men were more curious than anything else, but their curiosity brought them when pleas or even—perhaps especially—direct orders would not have.

Not enough, Slocum thought. He hurried next door to a plush saloon of the type not commonly visited by the lower classes and issued the same invitation there. Several of the customers in the saloon picked up their drinks and carried them into the sheriff's office also.

When enough were crowded into the small room, Slocum pushed his way through them to stand over Nate Smith.

"Look around you, Nate. Good men and true. Unlike your pal who's off finding you a doctor, these boys will be willing to listen to every word you have to tell them. And, Nate, I'll be right here listening too."

Smith looked truly afraid again for the first time since Slocum had carried him into the sheriff's office.

What had Fay said? That she did not trust Tom Atkins. She seemed to have had good reason for that reaction, Slocum thought. Because Nate Smith obviously *did* trust the county sheriff.

Fine. These good citizens of Trinidad would not be

so easily dismissed. Atkins could have ignored any complaints John Slocum might have lodged—unlikely as that would be, anyhow—but a confession made before a group of the town's citizens would be something else entirely.

"Tell them, Nate," Slocum ordered.

"What the hell is this all about?" one of the men grumbled. He looked as if he was about to turn and leave. He was a tall, handsome, very well dressed man, exactly the kind Slocum wanted to be listening.

"Wait," he said. "Nate?"

Smith swallowed. His eyes darted from Slocum to the well-dressed townsman and back again.

"Right here in front of these witnesses, Nate. Speak now, or you never will again. I swear it."

"You wouldn't."

"Try me." Slocum's hand went to the hilt of the knife at his hip. It would take no time at all. One swift slash, and he could be gone before any of the witnesses knew what he was up to. And Slocum had been chased before, by the best of them. Escape would not be a problem.

Apparently Smith could see his own death reflected in Slocum's hard eyes. The wounded man paled and in a choking voice said, "All right."

"Tell them."

Nate began, and once he started talking the disinterest in the eyes of the assembled men was gone. They crowded closer and listened intently to what he had to say.

"Why?" one of the men demanded.

For the first time since he had begun talking, Nate Smith's eyes left John Slocum.

"I was hired," he admitted. "I was paid to kill Trent."

"Who hired you?" The man who was asking the questions looked like a store clerk and was built the way blacksmiths are supposed to be. A real solid citizen, Slocum thought.

Smith shook his head. "I can't tell you that."

"I think you will," the clerk said.

"Never. I'm a lot of things, mister, but I'm not a fool."

"Bright had no part in it?" the same man asked.

"No," Smith admitted. "He was drunk and he was handy, that's all."

The townsman seemed to have taken control of the situation. Slocum was surprised. If he had had to guess beforehand, he would have pegged the better dressed fellow for that role.

"Harry," the clerk said to one of the other men, "the jail keys are hanging over there. You'd best let Bright out of his cell."

The man called Harry, who might have been a rancher from the way he was dressed, turned and did what he was told.

They brought Bright out. It was the first time Slocum had ever seen the young man. William was tall and thin, like his sister, and had her shade of hair coloring. He looked like any average young man who was trying to make his way in the world. He blinked in confusion when he was brought into the room, but brightened quickly when someone explained to him what had happened.

The sheriff and a smallish man carrying a black bag arrived in the midst of it all.

"What the hell is going on in my jail?" Atkins demanded loudly.

"Mr. Smith here just confessed to the murder William Bright was accused of," Slocum informed him with pleasure.

Atkins's eyes narrowed, but he got control of himself quickly and in front of the men who had placed him in office thanked Slocum for bringing in the murderer.

"That's all right, Sheriff. Just doing my public duty." There was laughter in Slocum's eyes, but he let none of it show on his face.

Other men were shoving their way into the jail now as the word spread. Atkins was red in the face, but there was nothing he could do in front of all these men to get back at Slocum.

A man Slocum thought he had seen before moved through the crowd to whisper something into Atkins's ear.

Too late Slocum realized just where he had seen that man before.

Atkins drew his revolver and snorted with pleasure.

"It's a grand day, boys," the sheriff said loudly. "Not only do we find the man who killed John Trent, but we also find the man who robbed Tim Cochran's payroll money a few weeks back." He pointed to Slocum. "That's him right there, boys."

Slocum thought about trying to shoot his way clear, but there was no room in the crowded office to run, and he was not even sure there was room to get his Colt into action. He stood quietly while a bunch of the men, including the clerk who was a natural leader among them, pinned his arms and stripped his weapons from him.

"Mind if I borrow your cell now that you won't be using it?" Slocum asked William Bright as he was forced out of the office and back toward the cells. Bright, a total stranger to him, just stood and stared as his benefactor was led away.

15

There were only two cells in the small jail. Slocum had one of them, and a heavily bandaged Nate Smith had the other. The doctor's opinion was that Smith would live to hang.

That was small comfort to Slocum. Nor was he particularly comfortable in other ways. After the excitement had died down, Sheriff Tom Atkins had paid him a visit. The sheriff had come calling when there were no witnesses except Smith, and Nate Smith certainly had no objections to what the sheriff had in mind.

"Come in, Sheriff," Slocum invited.

"In a minute," Atkins said. "Back around here to the bars. That's right. Now put your hands through. No—with your back to the bars so they're behind you. That's better."

Slocum felt the manacles being snapped around his wrists. The choice seemed to be to accept that or be shot, presumably while trying to escape.

"Feel safer now, Sheriff?"

"Uh-huh. I do." Atkins unlocked the barred door and entered his prisoner's cell. He laughed into Slocum's face.

"Tom Atkins," Slocum said. "Where have I heard that name before? I'm sure it wasn't as any damned lawman."

Atkins laughed again. "Ever been over Nevada way?"

"A time or two," Slocum admitted.

"Then you've likely heard of me," Atkins said with obvious pride.

"Shit," Slocum said. "Truckee Tom Atkins?"

"The same," the sheriff said.

"I reckon you can understand how I wouldn't've made the connection."

Atkins laughed. "I'll forgive you. For that, anyhow."

Truckee Tom Atkins had been known in certain limited circles as a specialist with a rifle for hire. Long-range assassination was his forte. For the right price he would free a mining claim of its annoying owners and open the way for someone else to claim it. He was said to have a nice little business built for himself over there.

"Whatever brought you over here, in this line of work?" Slocum asked.

The sheriff rubbed his face. "The eyes, actually. They started to go on me. Got to have good eyes for close work at long range. They build better rifles all the time, but none of them is worth a damn if you can't see the target."

"Pity," Slocum said.

"I agree. But I'm doing all right over here. The

money's good, and the work ain't hard" He grinned. "Sometimes, like right now, I really get to enjoy it."

"I don't suppose you'd consider a counter offer," Slocum said.

"No." Atkins went to work then, and he did seem to enjoy himself. He took his time about it and punched himself arm-weary using Slocum's belly for a punching bag.

The experience had hardly been pleasant, but Slocum was hardened and fit and the sheriff had become soft of muscle. Slocum had endured worse. And at least Atkins had removed the cuffs once he was tired and the jail cell door was securely locked once again with the sheriff out in the hall so Slocum could not get to him.

"I just wanted you to have something to think about," Atkins said.

Slocum let himself slump forward onto the cell's filthy floor and pretended he had passed out. He did not want to encourage a repeat performance.

Atkins let Slocum lie. He took a passing kick at his prisoner's head, but could not hit it well through the bars. He went on to the cell where Nate Smith was lying.

"The boss says you aren't to worry about anything, Nate," the sheriff said. "It's too late to lay Trent's killing on anyone else, of course, but the next best thing would be for you to get out of this part of the country."

"I'll do that, Tom. You know you can count on me."

"I know it, and the boss does too. He appreciates the way you kept your mouth shut today. He ain't likely to forget that."

"If I take a man's money, Tom, I won't peach on him. You can tell him that."

"Tell him yourself," Atkins said.

"He's coming here again?"

"No. He wouldn't want to be seen visiting you, but he's setting it up to spring you."

"When?"

"Tomorrow night. I can't be anywhere around, of course, so I'm gonna find some real important business to do somewhere out of town. Maybe a lead on the raiders that killed Cooper. We'll prob'ly pin that on you too after you're gone, but everyone knows there was a whole gang, so I'd still have a reason to be chasing the others." Atkins laughed. "I can say I got you to confess about your partners, and I'll take a posse into the hills after them. Soon as I'm gone, Jed and the boys will slip in here and take you out. If you like, they can make sure your cell mate over there doesn't draw a short sentence for his robbery."

Both of them laughed this time. Slocum lay with his eyes closed, listening to the bastards and wishing he could get his hands on a gun. Right now, with both of them handy, would be a good time for it.

"I don't know if I can ride, Tom. They might have to pack me out," Smith said. There was an edge of worry in his voice.

"I already talked to the doctor," Atkins assured him. "You're shot up, but you can make it. Hell, you got here alive, didn't you? Jed will take you back up to the cabin, and you can lay up there until you're ready to ride on your own. The boss said he'll give you a bonus before you leave. Then you can slip out of this part of the country, go down to Mexico, maybe. They say that's a real good place for a man to get his health back. Plenty of señoritas, and tequila ain't bad once you get used to it.''

"Sure. I've been there before," Smith said. "I know right where I want to go, too. I know some little señoritas there that are so hot they singe the hair right off a man's balls. Takes it a month to grow back in once you get this side of the border again.'' He laughed.

"Right," the sheriff said. "So don't you worry. It's all under control. Jed and the boys will be here sometime past midnight tomorrow night. You rest up and get to feeling better, hear?''

"I will, Tom, and I sure do thank you. Tell the boss I said so, will you? And tell him I won't never say a word to anyone about him. Never.''

"I'm real sure you won't," Atkins said.

Slocum could hear the sound of the outer door being closed and locked as Atkins left them alone.

Tomorrow night, Slocum thought.

If Nate Smith wanted to believe any of that horse-shit Atkins was trying to feed him, the man was the worst kind of fool.

Someone would come, all right, Probably not Jed; Jed really seemed to like Nate. Whoever this boss of theirs was, he was not likely to send Jed tomorrow

night. But someone would come. Only it would not
be one body they would leave behind; there would be
two: Slocum, as promised, and Nate Smith.

No smart man was going to trust Smith to keep his
mouth shut when he had already been scared once
into a confession. No way. The man had peached
once; he would do it again if a hangman's rope was
dangled in front of his eyes. Slocum was sure of that.
This boss would be too.

So they would come, exactly as promised, but
there would be no recuperation at the cabin. There
would be no possibility at all that someone might
discover Smith there and force a confession from
him.

That was all right, as far as it went. As far as
Slocum was concerned, Tom Atkins and his unknown
boss could hang Nate Smith twice and shoot him
three times more for good measure, and they wouldn't
hear a peep out of Slocum.

What distressed him was that they intended to
leave his blood pumping out onto a jail-cell floor at
the same time, damn them.

He thought about finding some way to have a word
with that clerk who had been willing to take charge
after Smith's confession.

But, damn it, the man would not listen to him
now. With the bad luck of being identified as the
payroll robber, anything he said now against the
good sheriff would be seen as just a way to throw
dust in the air and create confusion. It wasn't nearly
enough that he had brought Smith in and gotten his

confession. None of those men was likely now to believe anything John Slocum told them.

Damn, damn, damn!

Painfully, slowly, Slocum uncurled his body and pulled himself to the bunk that was his cell's only piece of furniture. He levered himself up into it and lay down. He felt somewhat better then. Not a whole lot, but some.

His mind kept racing.

There should be, there *had* to be, some way out of this cell before midnight tomorrow.

Unfortunately, he could not think of what it might be.

He closed his eyes and tried to sleep, or at least get some rest. If anything did come to him as a possible way out, he would need all the strength he could muster.

But all he could think about was the muzzle of a Colt .45, and himself locked behind bars while someone stood in the hallway and took potshots at him.

There isn't much room to run and hide in a jail cell.

16

Slocum would not recommend jail as the place for a restful interlude from the cares of the world. The food had been unfit to eat, although he had forced himself to eat it, and the sanitary conditions were unfit for hogs, although he used them as needed. All in all, it had been a miserable day.

What was worse, it was already well past dark, and while he had no watch or clock to tell him the time, he thought the hour was quickly moving toward midnight.

Slocum heard a scurrying of feet in the outer office and the sound of men's voices.

"Check those sons of bitches for me." It was the sheriff's voice.

A man he recognized as the clerk from the day before opened the door to look inside and make sure both prisoners were in their cells.

"You," Slocum said quickly. "You're an honest man. There's going to be a murder here tonight. Two of them. Mine and his both, while you're gone chasing ghosts. I heard the sheriff plan it last ni—"

The man shut the door on Slocum and locked it.

Just about what he had expected, Slocum figured.

Oh, come morning the bodies would be there, his and Nate Smith's, just like he had said. The man might remember what Slocum had said then. He might even be willing to do something about it. He probably would be, in fact. He really was an honest man.

But come morning it would be too late for that to make any difference to Slocum. If he was already cold beef, Slocum could not care less what happened.

He sighed and sat down on his bunk. Too late now for him even to try to convince Fay that she should bring him a gun, and give him a chance to defend himself anyway.

He had more than half expected to see her during the day. Her brother surely would have told her about how he had been sprung. She must have made the connection between William's benefactor and her lover, and surely she must have felt some gratitude.

On the ohter hand, Slocum admitted to himself now, maybe she had just been wanting to use him all along, for some bedstead exercise back there at her place, and for getting her brother out of the clink afterward.

No damn wonder she had not been upset when he told her about the life he had been leading before he met her. She wouldn't care about that. Likely she would not have cared if he had admitted to being Satan himself, just so her precious brother could be turned loose.

After that, it was old John's worry. Fay had what she wanted. Now Slocum could go hang or, in this particular matter, stand in the corner of a jail cell while a bunch of dumb yahoos filled him full of lead. So what? Slocum shook his head at his own gullibility. After all these years, a man would think he should have some judgement when he finally thought he had found a woman worth settling down with.

Stupid bastard. It probably served him right. All the damn women he had ridden away from, and now one had turned right around and screwed him, only to disappear without a backward look.

Slocum felt a little bitter about that. He figured he was entitled to.

"You were listening," he heard Nate Smith accuse him from his bunk in the next cell.

"I guess you proved it," Slocum said. "I'm no gentleman."

"You son of a bitch."

"Listen, I might be a son of a bitch, but at least I'm not a dumb shit like you are. You're so dumb you believed that crap Atkins handed you last night. Those boys aren't coming here to spring you, Smith. They're coming here to shoot you down. Then that wonderful boss of yours will know for sure that you won't talk."

"I wouldn't, and he knows it."

Slocum laughed bitterly. "Nate, if this was just one cell we was in and I could get a hand on you, by now I'd know everything you've ever heard, known, suspected, or been able to invent. I could make you talk about any damn thing in less than five minutes. Your boss knows that too.''

"Bullshit.''

Slocum grinned at him. "If you don't believe me, Nate, come over here to where I can reach you. I'll prove it to you when you hear yourself spill.''

Smith refused to answer him. He rolled to face the wall on his good side, his back to Slocum in the other cell.

Slocum stood. He had been examining the cell for most of the day, but he could not find anything he could use as a weapon against men armed with guns.

Still, a poor weapon was better than none at all.

His bunk was constructed of light lathing and cotton string, nothing heavy enough to do any real damage if a prisoner tried to tear it up and use it as a weapon. Slocum tore it up and selected the longest, strongest piece of wood he could find.

If those bastards wanted him, by damn, they would not find him crawling into a corner of the cell and waiting for them to shoot him down. He would be right up front to the last pulse of jetting blood, trying to brain at least one of the sons of bitches before he went down and out.

Smith laughed at him. "You don't have a chance,'' he taunted.

"The only difference between you and me in that,'' Slocum said, "is that I know it, and I am gonna try to do something about it. You'll just lie there and let them shoot you.''

"They're coming to spring me," Smith insisted. "Hell, old Jed wouldn't shoot me."

"Old Jed won't be here," Slocum promised. "Count on it."

"The boss couldn't get hold of any of the boys without me or Jed. I'm not so dumb as you think Slocum. I set it up that way on purpose. It has to be Jed coming, and Jed wouldn't kill me, no matter how much was offered."

Slocum shrugged. "Then it will be some other boys. Cantrell's is full of fellas who would shoot their wives if someone paid them fifty dollars."

"Cantrell's is full of boys who'd shoot their wives just to get rid of them," Smith said, "but my boss couldn't find Cantrell's neither without Jed. It takes a fella in the know to know about Cantrell's."

"You have an answer for everything, don't you, Nate?"

"Damn right I do."

"You think about that, then, when someone comes in here tonight an' empties a .45 into your belly. Maybe it will give you some satisfaction to know you're so damn right all the time."

"I was right about you," Nate said. "I knew better than to let Jed talk me into trusting you. I just wanted to keep an eye on you."

"It sure worked too. Got you shot all to pieces and about to be finished off."

Smith quit talking to him again.

Slocum hefted his flimsy bit of lathing. As a club

it would be next to useless. If he had a knife, he could sharpen the thing and make a spear of it.

But then, if he was going to wish for a knife, why not ask for a Colt instead, or a rifle. Hell, if you're wishing, wish for the best. Better yet, wish for a key to this stinking cell and be done with it.

Slocum did not have a key, but someone did. He had not heard the street door open, but now he could hear the faint clatter of keys on a ring as someone took the keys down from their peg in the sheriff's darkened office.

Slocum raised his bit of wood and hoped he could get at least one swing in before they killed him.

He was not afraid of the bastards. He was too busy being furious to think about fear. He just wanted to take one of them, any of them, with him.

The inner door swung open.

"John?"

It was Fay's voice.

"Here," he whispered. There probably was no reason in the world for him to be whispering, but he found himself doing it.

He heard a rustle of skirts as she came to him. She reached through the bars and crushed his hands to her own. She pressed her face against the bars and tried to kiss him.

"I thought you'd deserted me," Slocum said.

"Never." She was fumbling at the cell door with the ring of keys.

"Did you bring a gun?"

She nodded, and went on trying to make one of the keys fit the lock.

"Where?"

"Under my dress."

"Give it to me. Now."

"I almost . . ."

"Now," he insisted. If Smith's friends came, Slocum wanted to have a gun in his hand when they arrived. A pistol under Fay's dress would not be enough.

Besides himself to defend, he had to think about her safety now, too, and he would take no chances. But he could not suppress a great swelling of elation that rose within him.

All day long he had been wondering where Fay was, mentally accusing her of deserting him once she was done with him, thinking she had all of a sudden decided that her reputation was too fine to permit her to visit a robber in his cell.

Yet here she was, standing by him when he needed it most, and disregarding any risk to herself.

Fay quit trying to open the cell. She reached under her dress, dropping the ring of keys as she did so, but following Slocum's instructions.

She yanked the gun free from wherever she had been carrying it and thrust it through the bars into Slocum's hands. "It's the best I could find."

Slocum bit back the curse that rose to his lips. The pistol she handed him was an old pepperbox revolver. Five barrels, each with its separate charge of powder and ball and each with a shiny brass percussion cap.

As far as revolvers go, a pepperbox is a piece of crap. Less range and accuracy than a thrown cow chip. Less killing power than a bow and arrow.

But Slocum was delighted to have the fool thing. It sure beat the strip of lathing he had been prepared to use. He grabbed the little gun and grinned. Besides, somewhere in the outer office would be his own good Colt and his Winchester.

Once he could get his hands on those, no son of a bitch on earth could take him easy. Take him, maybe, but they would damn sure have to earn it.

Fay picked up the key ring and had to start all over trying to find the right one for the lock.

Slocum heard footsteps in the office. Probably William, he thought. He would likely be standing watch outside. Probably was wondering what was taking so long.

But the man who came to the door was not William Bright.

Slocum had seen him before. It was the very well dressed man who had been there the day before when Smith made his confession. What the hell was he doing here? He might have seen or heard something while he was passing by.

His tough luck, Slocum thought. But he couldn't be allowed to give the alarm until Fay and he were clear. Slocum raised the puny little pepperbox.

The man had a gun of his own in his hand, and he

was making no attempt at all to run away or shout for help.

"Thank God," Smith said from his bunk.

So *this was Smith's boss*.

Stupid Nate had been right about one thing: the boss had not been able to find a killer without Jed's knowledge. Not on such short notice.

He had come to do the job himself.

Slocum squeezed the trigger of the pepperbox. The lousy little pip-squeak thing misfired.

The boss raised his revolver with all the deliberation of an army lieutenant on the firing line, took careful aim, and shot Nate Smith in the head.

Slocum yanked the trigger of the pepperbox twice more, and heard only the dull sound of a hammer dropping onto metal.

The boss turned to face him.

Slocum continued to pull the trigger of the malfunctioning pepperbox. It fired twice, its round lead bullets wildly inaccurate.

Splinters flew from the door frame, but Slocum knew he had not connected with either shot.

The boss, whoever he was, snapped off a series of rapid shots, spraying the interior of the small jail before he ducked out of sight.

Slocum could have spit. When the man was no longer there, the lousy pepperbox decided to fire again. Its ball sped through an empty doorway into the sheriff's office, but the man was no longer in sight.

"Hurry, Fay, an' get this cell open."

He turned to her, and went utterly cold.

Fay Bright lay sprawled on the floor with her life's blood spraying from a ragged gash in her lovely throat.

"Oh . . . no!"

Slocum could hear shouts in the street beyond his cell window.

The sheriff was gone and so were most of the townsmen, racing on a false errand through the night, only Tom Atkins knowing where or why. But there would still be people in the town. They would be coming soon.

Slocum had no time to grieve.

Nor did he feel like grieving. Not now. There would be time enough for that later.

Now he only wanted to find and to kill the man who had shot down John Slocum's woman.

He bent and reached through the bars to recover the key ring. The iron was sticky with Fay's blood.

Slocum tried a key, and found it did not fit. There was little time left.

The second key went into the lock and turned easily. The tempered steel lock bar slid aside, and the door swung open to his touch.

Slocum paused for a second to look down at Fay. Her blood had ceased to flow, and her eyes stared glassily toward some distant place John Slocum had not yet visited.

He bent and took the time to straighten her dress.

She deserved better than to be shamed, even in death. Then he turned away from her without a backward look and raced for the office and his own good guns.

Slocum needed those guns now. He wanted to use them more than he ever had before. And there was no power on earth that could stop him.

17

Slocum made his way through the night to the livery and his roan. The hostler there took one look at the death in John Slocum's eyes and paled. The man saddled the horse without a word of protest and seemed anxious to have Slocum mounted and gone as quickly as possible.

That was understandable. Slocum was a walking arsenal when he left the sheriff's office. He had his own Colt and Winchester and he had taken along as well a spare Colt he found in Atkins's desk and a short-chopped, double-barreled shotgun with a bandolier of single-ought buckshot shells. With that he could chop a man in half at twenty paces or scythe through a mob at forty.

Even without any sort of weapon within his reach, though, any sensible man would have backed away from John Slocum that night. His jaw was set and his lips drawn thin. A murderous green fire lighted his eyes with the look of a Berserker seeking victims for his slaughter. That night, Slocum's gaze could have chilled the Devil.

He took the reins of his horse from the frightened

hostler and mounted with a swift, fluid motion. As soon as Slocum's back was turned he could hear the beat of running footsteps as the liveryman bolted out the back door of the barn. He felt no fear of that man or any other, and could not have cared less about the dangers of presenting his back to a stranger; if the man wanted to start something Slocum would be more than willing to oblige him.

Slocum rode boldly out of town toward the hills where his hunt would begin. Where it might end he neither knew nor cared. If he had to spend the next twenty years searching for the man who had shot Fay, he would do so. He cared nothing about speed now, only certainty. And he was absolutely certain that that man, whoever he was and wherever he ran, would pay with his life for a good woman's death.

He had gone less than three miles when he heard the clatter of approaching horses.

That many, riding toward the town, could only be the return of Sheriff Tom Atkins's alibi posse.

It would have been easy to turn the roan out of the road and slip into a stand of trees, or wait behind an outcropping of rock until the posse was safely past. But Slocum did not even consider it.

Instead he turned the roan sideways in the road, blocking the way as the posse members rode closer.

Finally they were near enough to see him. They came to a confused halt facing a lean, dark man who held a sawed-off shotgun in his right hand and a Colt revolver in his left.

"I want a word with you," Slocum said in a softly cold voice that carried to every man in the group.

Atkins, he saw with some satisfaction, was in the fore of the tired, dusty posse.

"Who . . .? *You!*" the sheriff choked.

"Me," Slocum agreed. "Surprised? You should be." To the other men he said, "Your good sheriff here was expecting me to be dead back in my cell tonight." He motioned with the muzzle of his revolver to the clerk he had tried to warn earlier. "I told you already," Slocum said.

"I still got no reason to believe anything you say," the clerk told him. "You've been caught escaping jail. Any man would lie at such a time."

Slocum laughed without mirth, and the sound of it was chilling. "Caught, eh? I expect you're right. I couldn't have heard the whole mob of you coming down this road. Couldn't possibly have slid off to the side while you went on by. I'd surely have been seen in all this good light. Wouldn't I?"

The clerk nodded reluctantly. "All right. You could have gotten away if you wanted to. So why did you stand there an' wait for us?"

"To tell you a little story," Slocum said, "and to get a man's name from you in return. A name and a location. I expect to have them."

"For a robber on the run from jail time," the clerk said, "I'll admit that you're bold."

"Don't you boys be listenin' to a single lie this thief has to tell you," Atkins warned. He was all too thoroughly aware of the direction the twin shotgun tubes were pointing. They were aimed unerringly at Atkins's belly. With every shift and dip of his fidgeting horse beneath Atkins, the shotgun muzzles tracked right on their target. It was making the sheriff pretty nervous.

"You remember what I told you a while ago?" Slocum asked the clerk.

"Of course."

"It happened, though not the way they'd planned. Nate Smith is dead in his locked cell. The poor bastard thought they were coming to take him out and free him. Instead he was shot through the head. The man who shot him tried to get me too. Instead he made the worst mistake he ever will get a chance to. He shot Miss Fay Bright instead, William Bright's sister. You boys all remember William. He's the young fellow you were all so hot to hang for a murder he hadn't done. Now his sister is dead. She bad come to the jail to thank me for helping her brother. A bullet was her reward for her kindness."

That story was thin and probably most of these posse members who were listening to it would realize the truth once they thought about it. But there seemed no point in compromising the reputation of a fine woman.

"The man who did the shooting is the same one who pays your sheriff here an extra salary for services rendered. He's the reason your sheriff took you out on a wild goose chase tonight. You didn't find anything from that hot tip of his tonight. You weren't supposed to. He used you so he'd have a good alibi for the slaughter in the jail tonight. Every one of you men would have to swear that Truckee Tom Atkins was with you when those murders were done. None of you could swear that Atkins knew they were gonna happen.''

Slocum looked at the sheriff and smiled a slow, ugly smile. "Boys," he said, "I can and do swear it.''

He looked again at the clerk, who was so obviously their natural, if unofficial, leader. "Did I see you react when I mentioned that name, mister? You heard me right. Your sheriff here is Truckee Tom Atkins.''

"I never thought. . . .''

"Course you didn't. A man wouldn't. And I'm betting—mind you, I wasn't here and couldn't know, but I'm sure betting—it was the same man who done those murders tonight that recommended his trusted friend Tom Atkins for the job of sheriff here.''

Atkins blinked. He looked nervously around at the men in the posse. Most, if not all, of them would have heard about Truckee Tom Atkins and his assassinations. Infamy was a necessary side effect of success in such a field, and he would know that better than most.

"That man," Slocum went on, "was there in the office when Smith was confessing. You remember him," he prompted. "Well dressed, handsome man, with a look of money about him.''

The clerk nodded. "I remember.''

"Who is he?''

The man swallowed. "If you aren't telling us the truth . . ."

"You'll know as soon as you get back to town, won't you?"

"We'll know."

"Who is he?"

"Blair. Andrew Blair."

"He's a big cheese around here?"

A nod.

"One of the two in the running for that coal contract?"

Another nod.

"And he's the man who brought Truckee Tom Atkins in to be your sheriff?"

"He did, but—"

"He did? That's enough for me to know. Where does this estimable Mr. Blair live?"

The clerk described the house.

"And his business?"

The man told him.

"Thank you, gentlemen. That's all I require of you tonight. You can go on now, if you like, except for Mr. Atkins there. I'd like him to stay and have a word with me."

"You can't—" Atkins began.

"I can, Tom, and I damn sure intend to. Matter of fact, I really don't give a shit if these gentlemen of the posse watch or not."

"It would be murder," Atkins said. There was a strong hint of a whine in his voice. "You know my eyes are going bad. You *know* that."

"It would be justice," Slocum said coldly. "These men—" he waved the Colt in a sweeping gesture to encompass the rest of the posse—"are welcome to call it what they want. I truly don't care. They can even join you in dying if that's what they want, Tom. They can't stop me. They can only go down with you."

"You can't do this to me, damn it."

"A man could make a lot of money taking up a wager on that, Tom," Slocum said calmly.

He motioned to the other men. "Those of you as wants to take a hand in this, stay right were you are. The rest of you might want to move out from behind. This gun don't exactly throw a narrow pattern, and I'd hate to take any of you by mistake."

There was a quick movement toward the sides of the road, and from the back of the posse Slocum could hear the hoofbeats of several horses in retreat into the night. No one stayed beside Sheriff Tom Atkins.

"A fair fight, Slocum. You owe me that much at least," Atkins begged.

"I *owe* you, Tom? For handcuffing me so you could beat me safely? But, hell, man, I can forget about that. I owe you, Tom? For participating in the death of the best and truest woman I've ever known? Tell me how that one works, Tom. Tell me how I owe you for that."

Atkins's mouth worked soundlessly for a moment. "That wasn't planned, you know. That wasn't supposed to happen at all."

"Wasn't planned, Tom? Wasn't supposed to happen? You're admitting then that this whole night's chase was faked to get you out of the jail and alibi your boss?"

"I am. I'm admitting all that, Slocum. I swear to God, I'll turn evidence on Blair. I'll help put him away. I'll go to jail myself. Just *please* don't murder me." Atkins looked wildly around at his posse members. "Don't let him do this, boys. Help me." He tried to grin at them. It came out as a ghastly rictus of pale lips and yellowed teeth. A trickle of drool ran out of the side of his mouth into his beard stubble.

"Look," Atkins said desperately, "I'm throwing my gun away now, boys. I'm surrendering. I'm surrendering to you, Jim." Jim seemed to be the name of the clerk. "Just don't let him kill me, Jim."

Atkins's left hand moved cautiously toward his belt buckle. He unsnapped it and let his gun belt fall free to the ground. Still Slocum sat and watched and waited.

"I'm not armed, boys. I've surrendered." He looked back toward Slocum. "You can't shoot me now, Slocum. I've surrendered. I'm unarmed. You can't shoot me now. And you know I could help you. I can help you convict Blair. I can put that son of a bitch in jail for the rest of his life. That's what you want, isn't it, Slocum? I can help you do it."

Slocum shook his head. "You do get confused about things, Tom. I don't want Andrew Blair in any jail. Why, I might not be able to get to him if he was. And you're wrong about something else too.

This bullshit about not shooting an unarmed man is for people who go by the rules. Me, Tom, I make my own rules. One of them is that there's a difference between a murder and an execution. In your case, Tom, I'd say what we have here is an execution.''

Slocum pulled the front trigger of the heavy-gauge shotgun, and the right barrel of the short gun gushed flame and smoke with an ear-splitting roar.

Truckee Tom Atkins was swept from his saddle, gouts of black blood spraying from a dozen ragged holes in his body.

A stray pellet caught his horse in the forehead and dropped it into the dust of the road as well.

None of the possemen moved, although several of their horses tried to bolt from the noise and the smoke and the sudden smell of fresh blood. Their riders brought the animals hurriedly back under control and sat with their hands well clear of their guns.

Slocum looked the men over. He honestly did not care if any of them tried him or not, and they must have seen that in his eyes and in the set of his shoulders, for none of them made any unnecessary motions at all.

Slocum nodded crisply. He nudged the roan forward and walked the animal slowly ahead until he was sitting high above the form of the bleeding sheriff.

The bastard wasn't dead yet, Slocum observed. It was unlikely that he would survive more than a few minutes longer, but a man never knew about a thing like that. Slocum had seen men absorb a fearsome amount of lead and live to tell about it, while others might die from an infected hangnail.

He looked into Atkins's clouding eyes and lowered the tubes of the shotgun over the man's face. Then he pulled the rear trigger.

"Good night, gentlemen," Slocum said.

He rode slowly away into what remained of the night. None of the possemen moved to stop or to follow him. Slocum turned his roan back toward Trinidad and Andrew Blair's house.

18

Slocum met the clerkish-looking man on the front porch of Blair's home. The dawn light was strong now, and daybreak would not be far behind.

"Jim, isn't it?" Slocum asked.

The man nodded. "Jim Tully."

"I hope they had the good sense to appoint you acting sheriff."

"They did, but we're going to run Rolfe Kuner in the special election."

Slocum stifled a yawn. "Blair isn't here, and I've already been to his office. The safe there is standing open. I figure he heard about it somehow, or guessed what would happen."

Jim Tully nodded again. "Things at the jail—well, you already know what we found there."

"Uh-huh. Did you come to arrest me?" Slocum looked amused by the thought.

"No. We aren't experts on the law, but we know some about common sense. She was your woman?"

"She was," Slocum said firmly. It was not a lie, he realized. Fay *had* been his woman, and he had been her man. More than even he had realized.

199

"I'm sorry, Slocum. I am truly sorry."

"I appreciate that, Sheriff Tully."

Tully smiled. "That's the first time I've been called that. It sounds strange."

"You'll do all right by it," Slocum said.

"Thank you." Tully looked startled. "Why should I be wanting your good opinion, Slocum? You're a robber. Technically speaking, I guess you're a murderer too."

"Who better to give you an opinion about a lawman, then?"

"You know," Tully said, "it probably wouldn't be a bad idea for you to get out of here before I have to do something official and stupid like try to take you in for a hearing or something." He rubbed his eyes. "I guess that's the kind of thing I'm supposed to do now."

"You have enough to do trying to get this part of the country cleaned up," Slocum said. "In case you're interested, Blair wasn't the only one trying to use hired guns to help his side of it. Blair's gang has been ambushed by the other side too. I wouldn't say that either bunch is clean."

Tully looked very tired. "Maybe we could talk the railroad into doing their own mining. I'll suggest it."

"You'll find some maps in Blair's desk," Slocum said. "I don't know much about such things, but I think they show where those coal reserves are. You could carry those along when you have your talk. It might help."

"Thanks for the suggestion."

"Yeah, well . . ." Slocum touched the brim of his hat. "I expect I'd better be getting along now. There's a man I have to see."

"If you find him, Slocum, I won't be able to protect you. Blair has some powerful friends."

The iciness had returned to Slocum's eyes. "He has some powerful enemies too."

Tully smiled. He hesitated for a moment, then shoved his hand forward. Slocum shook it.

"I hope you'll understand," the acting sheriff said, "if I tell you that I hope we don't meet again."

"I understand. Good luck to you, Jim Tully." Slocum turned and walked toward the roan that was tied at Blair's front gate.

The cabin was empty. There was no sign of Jed or any of Blair's men. The firebox was still hot, though, the chunks of aspen not yet completely burned, and aspen is a hot, quick-burning fuel. A half-full pot of coffee was on the stove. Slocum helped himself to a cup and found that it had not yet had time to become bitter with age.

There was no great hurry. Slocum would find them, as surely as the sun would set and rise again come morning. He rummaged through Jed's and the now dead Nate's supplies and cooked himself a huge breakfast. It had been a long night, and the future loomed infinitely long. He would want his strength when the time came to use it.

He ate and gave the roan some grain from a sack

he found in the hideout. When he was done, he rode
to Dewey Cantrell's.

"You aren't welcome here," Cantrell said when
Slocum walked through the door.

"You've heard, then? I'm glad." Slocum grinned
at the big man. "I was afraid I was going to have to
convince you first that I was serious. An' by the
way, if either hand leaves the surface of that bar,
Dewey, I'm gonna have to assume you're reaching
for a shotgun down there."

Cantrell grimaced, but he said nothing.

"Either of you boys work for Andrew Blair?"
Slocum asked the two men who were standing at the
far end of the bar.

"What's it to you?" one of them demanded.

"Anybody who rides for Blair," Slocum said, "I
figure to kill them, and Blair too."

"Oh." The man and his companion suddenly lost
interest in the pleasures of Dewey Cantrell's estab-
lishment. They turned away, leaving their drinks untouched on the bar before them, and walked out at a
pace just short of a trot.

Slocum watched them go, then drifted off to the
side away from the place where he had just been
standing. "Now, Cantrell," he said. "Tell me where
I might find Andrew Blair."

"I don't think so."

"It's a hard choice," Slocum said, "but you got
to make it." He smiled. "You got to decide which
one of us is going to be alive after I do find him.

And, Dewey, you got to be right the first time. You won't get a second chance.''

Cantrell swallowed hard. He looked undecided for a moment, then his shoulders sagged. ''I never peached on a man in my life.''

''Think of it this way, Dewey. I ain't the law. Matter of fact, I'm about the baddest son of a bitch in these hills. The law wouldn't have me except on the end of a rope.''

''All right.'' Cantrell looked unhappy. ''Mind if I pour myself a drink?''

''Just as long as your hands stay in sight.''

The big man nodded and reached for the neck of a bottle. As he picked it up, Slocum heard the rattle of beads as the fly curtain at the front door was brushed aside.

Slocum crouched and spun, his Colt in his hand, cocked before it cleared leather.

The two men who had just left the saloon were standing there with Winchesters in their hands.

Slocum shot first, and the nearer man sagged forward onto his knees with a .45 slug in his chest.

The other held his aim and fired before Slocum got off a second shot. Slocum's bullet ploughed through the hard walnut of the man's rifle stock to bury itself in the Blair rider's neck. Lead fragments and wood splinters combined with devastating effect, and the man was dead before what was left of his face hit the sawdust floor of the saloon.

''Shit,'' Slocum said aloud.

He turned and went to look down at the floor

behind the bar. Dewey Cantrell was dead too. The first man had been shooting at Slocum, the other at Cantrell. The second man had made his shot before Slocum was able to take him.

"Shit," he repeated. Three men who might have been able to point the way toward Andrew Blair, and now all of them were dead.

"Shit." He stalked out of the saloon in fury.

19

Slocum was tired and hungry. The few supplies he had carried on his saddle had been long since exhausted. He had been combing the mountains below Trinidad for several days now and had had no success there or in the choppy, rugged, rocky hills to the northwest, where the coal deposits were supposed to be. By now Andrew Blair could be a thousand rail miles away, and still Slocum had no lead on where he might have gone.

He scouted the hideout from the ridgetop where Jed had signaled with his lantern for the women that night, but Jim Tully seemed to be doing all too good a job as acting sheriff. There were two townsmen staying in the cabin. From the ridge, Slocum could see sunlight glint on the badges on their chests. Tully was after Blair too, it seemed.

Slocum thought about the women and their father. If the man was hungry for cash, Slocum could probably buy food there. He found the footpath leading to the place and scrambled his roan over it.

Shit, he thought. There was a deputy waiting there too. No doubt a very happy deputy.

Still, he wished Jim Tully was not as bright or as thorough as he was proving to be. Damn the man. Where was a venal, greedy, stupid lawman when you needed one? Slocum turned his roan away from the homestead and slipped away into the mountains unseen. His belly growled, and he felt a gnawing hunger that no amount of cold creek water or belt tightening was going to cure.

A beefsteak fried in tallow would go awfully good right now. Even a piece of damn pork. Or . . . he smiled . . . tortillas and beans.

He searched back through his memory. Carrera. Obregon Carrera. Slocum grinned and gigged the roan into a jog.

Slocum laid up in the cedars until it was nearly dark. He saw no deputies here, only Carrera and his sons coming home from their day's work. Señora Carrera and the little girl—he could not remember her name, although after being alone so long he could remember quite well the beginning bud-swell of her breasts in the sunlight the one time he had seen her before—were the only ones Slocum had seen around the place during the afternoon.

When he was reasonably sure there was no one there who did not belong, Slocum tightened his cinches and rode down to the jacal.

"Señor Slocum." Carrera was grinning broadly. "You honor us with a visit. You will stay?"

Slocum nodded. It was damn nice to be welcome somewhere. He had come awfully close to being permanently welcome somewhere. He put Fay out of his mind. "If I could buy some supper from you, I will."

"Buy? No. Eat with us, sí. It would be our pleasure." Carrera turned and spoke to his sons in rapid-fire Spanish. The boys jumped to take Slocum's horse and lead it away.

"The animal will be well cared for," Carrera promised. He chuckled. "It has had hard use, yes? Up, down, so many miles." Carrera motioned with his palm up and down the contours of the hills rising to the south and west. "We have a little grain, a little hay. The horse will eat well tonight. Come." He took Slocum by the arm and led him inside the tiny jacal.

As before, Slocum was treated royally. Señora Carrera heaped beans and shredded chicken onto an endless supply of torillas, and Slocum stuffed himself.

The little girl—Carmencita, he remembered finally—insisted on serving him. She hovered over him, stooping occasionally to deposit a soft kiss from her childish mouth onto his grizzled cheek.

Shit, Slocum chided himself, the day I get so hard up I abuse a kid like this, I might as well cut the damn thing off and pickle it, 'cause it wouldn't be no use any more.

She was a sweet child, and her happiness with life and living made him feel good. His eyes clouded when he wondered if Fay might have had that kind of pretty, happy child.

"That was fine," Slocum said when he could hold

no more. He wiped the grease from his chin with the back of his hand and patted his groaning stomach.

"Enough?" Carrera asked.

"More than enough. I appreciate it."

"Good."

"Something just occurred to me," Slocum said.

"Sí?"

"A little bit ago you were acting like you knew just where I'd been lately."

"But of course," Carrera said with an innocent smile. "My strong sons and I, we cut wood, sí? We take our wood to the town. We haul water from the clear springs to the houses so they do not have the taste of the river, sí? We go, we see, we listen. In the nights we tell each other the things we have seen and heard." Carrera grinned. "Your fine horse, he has lost the caulk on the right hind shoe, sí?"

Slocum nodded. The weld had torn, but the shoe was a good one and the missing caulk was not important.

"We know where you have been. We think you are looking for something or someone. Sometimes at night we make up things that you might be looking for. Gold, perhaps? We do not know of any or we would all be rich now and you would have a soft bed to sleep on tonight instead of a straw pad." He shrugged.

"Not gold," Slocum said. "A man named Andrew Blair."

"I know him," Carrera said. "I sold water at his house. He does not like to wash his face in the river water, even. He was a good . . . customer?" He seemed uncertain of the word.

Slocum nodded.

"Now he is gone from the house," Carrera said. "A pity. Now he has no need of my water."

"He doesn't need it now?"

Carrera shrugged. "Not with a spring so near. Of course he does not."

"So . . . *a spring so near to where?*" Slocum was on his feet. His voice was loud, and the Carrera family recoiled from him.

"I'm sorry," Slocum said. "I didn't mean to shout. But, damn it, Obregon, this is important to me. Do you mean to tell me you know where Andrew Blair is hiding out?"

"Of course," Carrera said. He looked as if that was only to be expected. Hadn't he just told Slocum that he and his sons knew the tracks on all of these mountains?

"Where?" Slocum pleaded.

"You know the place where you stayed with the hombres who worked for this man?"

"The cabin? Hell, yes."

"Above it there is another cabin, very old, in another, smaller bowl higher on the mountain. Horses cannot go there, but a man can climb to it. They are there."

"Still there? You're sure?"

Carrera shrugged. "Who is sure? But I think this is true. There are other men staying in the cabin where you once slept. I think this Señor Blair does

not want to go past them. He would have to do this
to leave. I think he is still there. It has been—'' he
stopped and spoke with his sons for a moment—''it
has been, I think, three days since we were there
collecting pinon nuts. Very good flour, pinon. Indi-
ans and Mexicans know this, and it costs nothing but
the work of collecting the nuts.''

Slocum did not give a shit about the damn nuts,
but he forced himself to be calm. ''Tell me how to
get there, Obregon. Please.''

Carrera shrugged. ''It is simple.''

Slocum held his Winchester carefully to keep from
banging the stock onto a rock and giving him away.
The climb down from the pinons into the tiny bowl
was slow but not particularly dangerous from where
Carrera had told him to start. Climbing up the rocky
chute from the cirque where Jed's hole-up was would
have been another matter. It would have been impossible to do that quietly.

Even knowing it was there, it had taken Slocum
several minutes of close study to find the opening of
the cabin Carrera had told him about.

According to the Mexican, it had been occupied by
a trapper a very long time ago. It was a rock overhang, not exactly a cave, but close to it, that had
been walled with timbers to make a shelter.

Slocum could see no smoke to tell him the place
was being used, but with Tully's deputies so close
below on the mountainside he would not have expected any. If Blair and any of his men were still

there, they must have been having an uncomfortable time of it stuck there with some unsuspecting deputies in the bottleneck of their little hiding place.

He reached the bottom of the bowl and thumbed the hammer of the Winchester back. There was already a cartridge in the chamber. He checked to make sure his Colt was free in its leather.

Slocum grinned. There was no door on the ancient cabin, and a blanket had been tacked over the entrance to keep the wind out. A blanket would have rotted away quickly, so it had to be new. And surely anyone leaving the place would have taken it along with them. The odds were looking better that Carrera had been right: that Blair and, Carrera had thought, two other men were still in residence.

Slocum had no intention of entering the cabin. Showing himself in the doorway would have been a fine way to commit suicide, but he was in the market for a different result.

On the other hand, give him a few minutes up here and he could not care less if Tully's boys were alerted and climbed up to see what they had been living underneath the last little while. Slocum crept up beside the windowless front and only wall of the little cabin and grinned. He took out a cigar and lighted it. He used the same match to touch off the dry, seasoned timbers the wall was built from. When the flame was well caught he stepped back and waited.

Within minutes he heard coughing and a fair amount of fancy cussing. Three men came tumbling out into the light, rubbing their eyes and grumbling.

"Which one of you dumb bastards—" Blair began. He cut the sentence short when he saw Slocum squared off in front of him.

"You look the worse for wear, Andrew," Slocum said pleasantly.

He was right. Andrew Blair's shirt had lost its collar and had acquired a layer of grime on what once had been a laundered and crisply starched article. Blair had not shaved recently, and his hair was an unkempt tangle. He did not look at all the fine gentleman Slocum remembered seeing before.

"You!"

"Surely you didn't think I wouldn't find you." Slocum nodded to the two men who had stuck with their boss when his bubble burst. "Jed," he said, "good to see you again. And you, Perry."

Blair looked frightened. "Kill him," he ordered.

"Jed," Slocum said, "I kinda got to liking you, and it ain't you I want, just him." He hooked a thumb toward Blair. "If you and Newcombe want to slope out of here, I won't be following you."

Jed looked toward Blair and then back to Slocum. He smiled. "I don't want to fight with you, John. You saved my butt once. I wouldn't forget that even if I didn't like you, which I reckon I do." He turned to Blair. "Sorry, boss, but that's the way it is. There's no percentage in working for a dead man."

Jed reached to unbuckle his gun belt, but Slocum stopped him. "Keep it, Jed. There's some deputies down below. You might need that thing to get out past them."

The outlaw's eyes widened. "You'd trust me, John?"

Slocum shrugged. "In a way, Jed. I also figure I could take you if you tried to double back on me. But I don't figure you for the kind of man who'd do that."

"Thank you, John. And if we meet again . . . ?"

"No hard feelings," Slocum assured him. "We'll have a drink together."

Jed smiled and hurried away. Slocum did not bother to watch him go. He could hear Jed's footsteps until he was out of effective pistol range.

"Perry?" Slocum asked. "Like I told Jed, my quarrel is with Mr. Blair here. I've heard some good things about you, boy. I'd hate to see you go out trying to side a shit like this one."

"Terribly sorry, sir," Newcombe said with his polite manner. "I accepted the gentleman's pay, don't you know."

"Like Jed said, boy, you can't work for a dead man."

"*Kill him!*" Blair screamed.

Perry Newcombe sighed. "I *am* quite competent, Mr. Slocum. And it shall do me no harm to be known as the man who bested you in a fair fight."

"Suit yourself, boy, but don't take too long about it. I'm wanting to concentrate on Mr. Blair here. Him and me, we got an awful lot to talk about, an' I think it might take him a long time to die."

Newcombe tensed, his right hand curling over the grip of his revolver. Slocum stood, relaxed and steady.

He let his right hand fall away from the stock of his
Winchester so it was free to hook his .45 out. Other
than that, an observer would not have known that he
was preparing himself for a life-or-death race with
the young Englishman.

"After you, sir," Newcombe said. A vein in the
side of his neck was pulsing visibly, and the tension
had started a tic fluttering at his left eye.

"I sure wish you'd walk away and go out with
Jed," Slocum said. "You're too nice a young fellow
to waste on the likes of this trash."

"I am sure you would wish me to bow out, but
you must earn the privilege, sir."

Slocum grinned. "I've said the like myself a time
or two, boy, but never so fancy as that."

The wall of the old cabin was flaming fiercely
now, and the heat extended far into the bowl. There
was as yet little smoke from the long-dried wood,
though, and there seemed to be no outcry from below.

"Kill him *now!*" Andrew Blair shrieked.

The sound of Blair's voice was signal enough.

Perry Newcombe was unbelievably fast with his
hands. His slim, weak-looking fingers had the speed
of a striking snake, and he got his shot off before
Slocum's .45 was fully clear of the leather.

The youngster was fast, probably better than anyone John Slocum had ever faced—but Slocum was
both fast and accurate.

Slocum's slug took Newcombe in the stomach,
and the Englishman's muzzle sagged so that his second shot went into the dirt between them.

Slocum shot again, this time into Newcombe's chest, then a finishing shot as he went down.

"Like the man said," Slocum muttered, "a fast noise ain't killed nobody."

Andrew Blair went fish-belly pale. He dropped to his knees and began to plead with Slocum.

Slocum did not pay attention to any of the things the man was babbling about.

There was something about money. Slocum laughed while Blair ripped open his soiled shirt and yanked a money belt from around his waist. Blair threw the belt at Slocum's feet and began to cry. The tears were making shiny, wet, somewhat cleaner tracks on the man's grimy face.

"I've been real eager for this," Slocum said darkly. "Just you and me, Andrew, and enough time for you to die remembering a woman who done you no harm."

Blair's shoulders were heaving from his sobs. He groveled on the ground and begged Slocum not to harm him.

Slocum holstered his Colt, and laid the Winchester aside, and pulled his knife.

He stepped forward and knelt beside the hysterical man.

"Time to pay the piper," Slocum said. His voice was gentle, but there was no mercy in his eyes as he bent forward and made the first of many slices.

20

Fat Nellie came hurrying down the hall of the Stockman's Delights. She was giggling and carrying a basin of soapy water.

"What, another one?" the madam asked with disbelief.

"Another one," Fat Nellie said with another giggle. "And another bottle too."

"He is paying up front, ain't he?" the madam asked.

Fat Nellie laughed. "You should see the money belt he's got."

"How much is in it?"

"Lordy, don't ask me! He's got a pistol layin' on top of the thing an' a knife beside that. Don't you go asking *me* to check his poke."

The madam smiled. "That's all right, darlin', we're doing just fine without that."

"He said he wants another girl too," the whore admitted. "Someone bigger than me if you can round one up for him. Said he wants a lot of meat to waller on. No skinny women, or he'll . . . well, he didn't exactly say what he'd do. But I don't think we want to find out. Anyway, he has somethin' in mind that'll take several of us, and he says he wants a short, plump girl that can go the distance with him.''

The madam thought for a moment. "I could borrow Miss Polly's Emmaline, but that old bitch would charge me an arm and two legs for the loan. What do you think, Nellie?''

Fat Nellie paused and wiped at a line of sweat rolling down between her massive, sagging tits. The sweat tickled. "Baby Marie over at the Star Bright? Besides, Marie will go along with any damn thing, and this john looks like he could be nasty if he wanted to.''

"He hasn't damaged you, has he?" the madam asked, quick concern for the next week's profits in her voice.

"No, he ain't done anything, exactly. It's just— well—somethin' in his eyes. An' the way he keeps drinkin' without it doing anything to him. He ain't a natural man, somehow. I don't know how to tell you. Just . . . something.''

The madam nodded. "You had a good idea, Nellie. I'll send someone over to borrow Baby Marie. You go ahead and get the bottle he wants and take it in to him. And, mind you, anything he wants, long as he pays for it, you see that you an' Marie give it to him. Just make sure if he wants to get rough he knows that costs extra.''

"Yes'm." Fat Nellie sighed. "Poor man.''

"What?''

"Nothing, ma'am, nothing at all. Just a feelin' I

got somehow.'' The chubby whore went hurrying back down the hallway toward the room and the waiting customer. She was eager to take his money and, perhaps incidentally, to help him forget whatever it was he seemed to be trying to get over.

She shook her head. It wasn't like her to care anything about her customers. It wasn't professional. She would have to learn to get over that.

She stopped at the door for a moment and pasted a smile onto her round face. She was giggling again when she opened the door and went inside. Fat girls are always supposed to be jolly, and this man certainly seemed to want to be jollied. If that was what he wanted, why, she would sure give it to him. Just as long as that money belt held out, the poor bastard could have anything he wanted.

She just didn't understand, though, why nothing she could do for him ever seemed to be quite enough to satisfy.

JAKE LOGAN